SO SMITTEN

(A Faith Bold Mystery —Book Ten)

BLAKE PIERCE

Blake Pierce

Blake Pierce is the USA Today bestselling author of the RILEY PAGE mystery series, which includes seventeen books. Blake Pierce is also the author of the MACKENZIE WHITE mystery series, comprising fourteen books; of the AVERY BLACK mystery series, comprising six books; of the KERI LOCKE mystery series, comprising five books; of the MAKING OF RILEY PAIGE mystery series, comprising six books; of the KATE WISE mystery series, comprising seven books; of the CHLOE FINE psychological suspense mystery, comprising six books; of the JESSIE HUNT psychological suspense thriller series, comprising thirty-five books (and counting); of the AU PAIR psychological suspense thriller series, comprising three books; of the ZOE PRIME mystery series, comprising six books; of the ADELE SHARP mystery series, comprising sixteen books, of the EUROPEAN VOYAGE cozy mystery series, comprising six books; of the LAURA FROST FBI suspense thriller, comprising eleven books; of the ELLA DARK FBI suspense thriller, comprising twenty-one books (and counting); of the A YEAR IN EUROPE cozy mystery series, comprising nine books, of the AVA GOLD mystery series, comprising six books; of the RACHEL GIFT mystery series, comprising thirteen books (and counting); of the VALERIE LAW mystery series, comprising nine books; of the PAIGE KING mystery series, comprising eight books; of the MAY MOORE mystery series, comprising eleven books; of the CORA SHIELDS mystery series, comprising eight books; of the NICKY LYONS mystery series, comprising eight books, of the CAMI LARK mystery series, comprising ten books; of the AMBER YOUNG mystery series, comprising seven books (and counting); of the DAISY FORTUNE mystery series, comprising five books; of the FIONA RED mystery series, comprising eleven books (and counting); of the FAITH BOLD mystery series, comprising eleven books (and counting); of the JULIETTE HART mystery series, comprising five books (and counting); of the MORGAN CROSS mystery series, comprising nine books (and counting); of the FINN WRIGHT mystery series, comprising five books (and counting); of the new SHEILA STONE suspense thriller series, comprising five books (and counting); and of the new RACHEL BLACKWOOD suspense thriller series, comprising five books (and counting).

An avid reader and lifelong fan of the mystery and thriller genres,

Blake loves to hear from you, so please feel free to visit www.blakepierceauthor.com to learn more and stay in touch.

ISBN: 978-1-0943-8362-0

BOOKS BY BLAKE PIERCE

RACHEL BLACKWOOD SUSPENSE THRILLER
NOT THIS WAY (Book #1)
NOT THIS TIME (Book #2)
NOT THIS CLOSE (Book #3)
NOT THIS ROAD (Book #4)
NOT THIS LATE (Book #5)

SHEILA STONE SUSPENSE THRILLER
SILENT GIRL (Book #1)
SILENT TRAIL (Book #2)
SILENT NIGHT (Book #3)
SILENT HOUSE (Book #4)
SILENT SCREAM (Book #5)

FINN WRIGHT MYSTERY SERIES
WHEN YOU'RE MINE (Book #1)
WHEN YOU'RE SAFE (Book #2)
WHEN YOU'RE CLOSE (Book #3)
WHEN YOU'RE SLEEPING (Book #4)
WHEN YOU'RE SANE (Book #5)

MORGAN CROSS MYSTERY SERIES
FOR YOU (Book #1)
FOR RAGE (Book #2)
FOR LUST (Book #3)
FOR WRATH (Book #4)
FOREVER (Book #5)
FOR US (Book #6)
FOR NOW (Book #7)
FOR ONCE (Book #8)
FOR ETERNITY (Book #9)

JULIETTE HART MYSTERY SERIES
NOTHING TO FEAR (Book #1)
NOTHING THERE (Book #2)
NOTHING WATCHING (Book #3)

NOTHING HIDING (Book #4)
NOTHING LEFT (Book #5)

FAITH BOLD MYSTERY SERIES
SO LONG (Book #1)
SO COLD (Book #2)
SO SCARED (Book #3)
SO NORMAL (Book #4)
SO FAR GONE (Book #5)
SO LOST (Book #6)
SO ALONE (Book #7)
SO FORGOTTEN (Book #8)
SO INSANE (Book #9)
SO SMITTEN (Book #10)
SO SIMPLE (Book #11)

FIONA RED MYSTERY SERIES
LET HER GO (Book #1)
LET HER BE (Book #2)
LET HER HOPE (Book #3)
LET HER WISH (Book #4)
LET HER LIVE (Book #5)
LET HER RUN (Book #6)
LET HER HIDE (Book #7)
LET HER BELIEVE (Book #8)
LET HER FORGET (Book #9)
LET HER TRY (Book #10)
LET HER PLAY (Book #11)

DAISY FORTUNE MYSTERY SERIES
NEED YOU (Book #1)
CLAIM YOU (Book #2)
CRAVE YOU (Book #3)
CHOOSE YOU (Book #4)
CHASE YOU (Book #5)

AMBER YOUNG MYSTERY SERIES
ABSENT PITY (Book #1)
ABSENT REMORSE (Book #2)
ABSENT FEELING (Book #3)
ABSENT MERCY (Book #4)

ABSENT REASON (Book #5)
ABSENT SANITY (Book #6)
ABSENT LIFE (Book #7)

CAMI LARK MYSTERY SERIES
JUST ME (Book #1)
JUST OUTSIDE (Book #2)
JUST RIGHT (Book #3)
JUST FORGET (Book #4)
JUST ONCE (Book #5)
JUST HIDE (Book #6)
JUST NOW (Book #7)
JUST HOPE (Book #8)
JUST LEAVE (Book #9)
JUST TONIGHT (Book #10)

NICKY LYONS MYSTERY SERIES
ALL MINE (Book #1)
ALL HIS (Book #2)
ALL HE SEES (Book #3)
ALL ALONE (Book #4)
ALL FOR ONE (Book #5)
ALL HE TAKES (Book #6)
ALL FOR ME (Book #7)
ALL IN (Book #8)

CORA SHIELDS MYSTERY SERIES
UNDONE (Book #1)
UNWANTED (Book #2)
UNHINGED (Book #3)
UNSAID (Book #4)
UNGLUED (Book #5)
UNSTABLE (Book #6)
UNKNOWN (Book #7)
UNAWARE (Book #8)

MAY MOORE SUSPENSE THRILLER
NEVER RUN (Book #1)
NEVER TELL (Book #2)
NEVER LIVE (Book #3)
NEVER HIDE (Book #4)

NEVER FORGIVE (Book #5)
NEVER AGAIN (Book #6)
NEVER LOOK BACK (Book #7)
NEVER FORGET (Book #8)
NEVER LET GO (Book #9)
NEVER PRETEND (Book #10)
NEVER HESITATE (Book #11)

PAIGE KING MYSTERY SERIES
THE GIRL HE PINED (Book #1)
THE GIRL HE CHOSE (Book #2)
THE GIRL HE TOOK (Book #3)
THE GIRL HE WISHED (Book #4)
THE GIRL HE CROWNED (Book #5)
THE GIRL HE WATCHED (Book #6)
THE GIRL HE WANTED (Book #7)
THE GIRL HE CLAIMED (Book #8)

VALERIE LAW MYSTERY SERIES
NO MERCY (Book #1)
NO PITY (Book #2)
NO FEAR (Book #3)
NO SLEEP (Book #4)
NO QUARTER (Book #5)
NO CHANCE (Book #6)
NO REFUGE (Book #7)
NO GRACE (Book #8)
NO ESCAPE (Book #9)

RACHEL GIFT MYSTERY SERIES
HER LAST WISH (Book #1)
HER LAST CHANCE (Book #2)
HER LAST HOPE (Book #3)
HER LAST FEAR (Book #4)
HER LAST CHOICE (Book #5)
HER LAST BREATH (Book #6)
HER LAST MISTAKE (Book #7)
HER LAST DESIRE (Book #8)
HER LAST REGRET (Book #9)
HER LAST HOUR (Book #10)
HER LAST SHOT (Book #11)

HER LAST PRAYER (Book #12)
HER LAST LIE (Book #13)

AVA GOLD MYSTERY SERIES
CITY OF PREY (Book #1)
CITY OF FEAR (Book #2)
CITY OF BONES (Book #3)
CITY OF GHOSTS (Book #4)
CITY OF DEATH (Book #5)
CITY OF VICE (Book #6)

A YEAR IN EUROPE
A MURDER IN PARIS (Book #1)
DEATH IN FLORENCE (Book #2)
VENGEANCE IN VIENNA (Book #3)
A FATALITY IN SPAIN (Book #4)

ELLA DARK FBI SUSPENSE THRILLER
GIRL, ALONE (Book #1)
GIRL, TAKEN (Book #2)
GIRL, HUNTED (Book #3)
GIRL, SILENCED (Book #4)
GIRL, VANISHED (Book 5)
GIRL ERASED (Book #6)
GIRL, FORSAKEN (Book #7)
GIRL, TRAPPED (Book #8)
GIRL, EXPENDABLE (Book #9)
GIRL, ESCAPED (Book #10)
GIRL, HIS (Book #11)
GIRL, LURED (Book #12)
GIRL, MISSING (Book #13)
GIRL, UNKNOWN (Book #14)
GIRL, DECEIVED (Book #15)
GIRL, FORLORN (Book #16)
GIRL, REMADE (Book #17)
GIRL, BETRAYED (Book #18)
GIRL, BOUND (Book #19)
GIRL, REFORMED (Book #20)
GIRL, REBORN (Book #21)

LAURA FROST FBI SUSPENSE THRILLER

ALREADY GONE (Book #1)
ALREADY SEEN (Book #2)
ALREADY TRAPPED (Book #3)
ALREADY MISSING (Book #4)
ALREADY DEAD (Book #5)
ALREADY TAKEN (Book #6)
ALREADY CHOSEN (Book #7)
ALREADY LOST (Book #8)
ALREADY HIS (Book #9)
ALREADY LURED (Book #10)
ALREADY COLD (Book #11)

EUROPEAN VOYAGE COZY MYSTERY SERIES
MURDER (AND BAKLAVA) (Book #1)
DEATH (AND APPLE STRUDEL) (Book #2)
CRIME (AND LAGER) (Book #3)
MISFORTUNE (AND GOUDA) (Book #4)
CALAMITY (AND A DANISH) (Book #5)
MAYHEM (AND HERRING) (Book #6)

ADELE SHARP MYSTERY SERIES
LEFT TO DIE (Book #1)
LEFT TO RUN (Book #2)
LEFT TO HIDE (Book #3)
LEFT TO KILL (Book #4)
LEFT TO MURDER (Book #5)
LEFT TO ENVY (Book #6)
LEFT TO LAPSE (Book #7)
LEFT TO VANISH (Book #8)
LEFT TO HUNT (Book #9)
LEFT TO FEAR (Book #10)
LEFT TO PREY (Book #11)
LEFT TO LURE (Book #12)
LEFT TO CRAVE (Book #13)
LEFT TO LOATHE (Book #14)
LEFT TO HARM (Book #15)
LEFT TO RUIN (Book #16)

THE AU PAIR SERIES
ALMOST GONE (Book#1)
ALMOST LOST (Book #2)

ALMOST DEAD (Book #3)

ZOE PRIME MYSTERY SERIES
FACE OF DEATH (Book#1)
FACE OF MURDER (Book #2)
FACE OF FEAR (Book #3)
FACE OF MADNESS (Book #4)
FACE OF FURY (Book #5)
FACE OF DARKNESS (Book #6)

A JESSIE HUNT PSYCHOLOGICAL SUSPENSE SERIES
THE PERFECT WIFE (Book #1)
THE PERFECT BLOCK (Book #2)
THE PERFECT HOUSE (Book #3)
THE PERFECT SMILE (Book #4)
THE PERFECT LIE (Book #5)
THE PERFECT LOOK (Book #6)
THE PERFECT AFFAIR (Book #7)
THE PERFECT ALIBI (Book #8)
THE PERFECT NEIGHBOR (Book #9)
THE PERFECT DISGUISE (Book #10)
THE PERFECT SECRET (Book #11)
THE PERFECT FAÇADE (Book #12)
THE PERFECT IMPRESSION (Book #13)
THE PERFECT DECEIT (Book #14)
THE PERFECT MISTRESS (Book #15)
THE PERFECT IMAGE (Book #16)
THE PERFECT VEIL (Book #17)
THE PERFECT INDISCRETION (Book #18)
THE PERFECT RUMOR (Book #19)
THE PERFECT COUPLE (Book #20)
THE PERFECT MURDER (Book #21)
THE PERFECT HUSBAND (Book #22)
THE PERFECT SCANDAL (Book #23)
THE PERFECT MASK (Book #24)
THE PERFECT RUSE (Book #25)
THE PERFECT VENEER (Book #26)
THE PERFECT PEOPLE (Book #27)
THE PERFECT WITNESS (Book #28)
THE PERFECT APPEARANCE (Book #29)
THE PERFECT TRAP (Book #30)

THE PERFECT EXPRESSION (Book #31)
THE PERFECT ACCOMPLICE (Book #32)
THE PERFECT SHOW (Book #33)
THE PERFECT POISE (Book #34)
THE PERFECT CROWD (Book #35)

CHLOE FINE PSYCHOLOGICAL SUSPENSE SERIES
NEXT DOOR (Book #1)
A NEIGHBOR'S LIE (Book #2)
CUL DE SAC (Book #3)
SILENT NEIGHBOR (Book #4)
HOMECOMING (Book #5)
TINTED WINDOWS (Book #6)

KATE WISE MYSTERY SERIES
IF SHE KNEW (Book #1)
IF SHE SAW (Book #2)
IF SHE RAN (Book #3)
IF SHE HID (Book #4)
IF SHE FLED (Book #5)
IF SHE FEARED (Book #6)
IF SHE HEARD (Book #7)

THE MAKING OF RILEY PAIGE SERIES
WATCHING (Book #1)
WAITING (Book #2)
LURING (Book #3)
TAKING (Book #4)
STALKING (Book #5)
KILLING (Book #6)

RILEY PAIGE MYSTERY SERIES
ONCE GONE (Book #1)
ONCE TAKEN (Book #2)
ONCE CRAVED (Book #3)
ONCE LURED (Book #4)
ONCE HUNTED (Book #5)
ONCE PINED (Book #6)
ONCE FORSAKEN (Book #7)
ONCE COLD (Book #8)
ONCE STALKED (Book #9)

ONCE LOST (Book #10)
ONCE BURIED (Book #11)
ONCE BOUND (Book #12)
ONCE TRAPPED (Book #13)
ONCE DORMANT (Book #14)
ONCE SHUNNED (Book #15)
ONCE MISSED (Book #16)
ONCE CHOSEN (Book #17)

MACKENZIE WHITE MYSTERY SERIES
BEFORE HE KILLS (Book #1)
BEFORE HE SEES (Book #2)
BEFORE HE COVETS (Book #3)
BEFORE HE TAKES (Book #4)
BEFORE HE NEEDS (Book #5)
BEFORE HE FEELS (Book #6)
BEFORE HE SINS (Book #7)
BEFORE HE HUNTS (Book #8)
BEFORE HE PREYS (Book #9)
BEFORE HE LONGS (Book #10)
BEFORE HE LAPSES (Book #11)
BEFORE HE ENVIES (Book #12)
BEFORE HE STALKS (Book #13)
BEFORE HE HARMS (Book #14)

AVERY BLACK MYSTERY SERIES
CAUSE TO KILL (Book #1)
CAUSE TO RUN (Book #2)
CAUSE TO HIDE (Book #3)
CAUSE TO FEAR (Book #4)
CAUSE TO SAVE (Book #5)
CAUSE TO DREAD (Book #6)

KERI LOCKE MYSTERY SERIES
A TRACE OF DEATH (Book #1)
A TRACE OF MURDER (Book #2)
A TRACE OF VICE (Book #3)
A TRACE OF CRIME (Book #4)
A TRACE OF HOPE (Book #5)

PROLOGUE

All in all, Vinny liked his job. It wasn't a glamorous job, not even in the world of the criminal underground, but that was one of the things Vinny liked. He didn't need to worry about a price on his head or a target on his back. As long as he stayed in the shadows, he would be allowed to remain in the shadows, and if things ever got too heavy like they had in Boston, he could just fade away and disappear. In the meantime, he could make a lot of money doing relatively light work.

It was a good life for a thief.

Today would be even lighter work than usual. The gang didn't need any more fighting dogs for a while. That meant no body armor, no stun guns, no spiked collars and more importantly, no having to wonder if the dog he was kidnapping would get past all of his defenses and just rip him to pieces. He remembered reading about a case a while back where some cuckoo in Arizona was siccing dogs on people and tearing them to pieces. Not a good way to go, no sirree. No good for Vinny.

Today, he didn't need to worry about that. The gang needed bait dogs, sweet, innocent little things that wouldn't hurt a fly. Preferably animals that *couldn't* hurt a fly.

That suited Vinny just fine. He got paid less for bait dogs, but he could pull four or five of those on a good night. Fighting dogs were always one at a time and much harder work.

He strolled down the neighborhood whistling. He wasn't worried about being seen. This was the sort of neighborhood where people wore blinders. What wasn't their business couldn't hurt them. That was the prevailing attitude in the projects, and that also suited Vinny just fine.

That didn't mean he could be brazen, but it did mean that he could work without fear that some nosy neighbor would call the police on him. Vinny had watched the neighborhood for a few weeks now, and he knew the owner wouldn't arrive for several hours.

It paid to know things. That was another thing Vinny was good at. In Boston, knowing things had allowed Vinny to obtain a position of some prestige in the Franco family. Vinny no longer made it his business to sell information, but he still liked knowing things. Knowing things kept men like him alive.

He reached the house and noted the chainlink fence that encircled the front yard. He glanced casually to his right and saw that the same fence wrapped around the backyard as well, separated by a decrepit wooden gate. He tapped the wire cutters in his pocket and continued down the street.

When he reached the end, he turned right, then right again. The houses on Becker Street were separated from the houses on Grant Street by a two-foot-wide easement that at one point served as a concrete-lined drainage ditch, but now served as an overgrown pile of dirt with five-foot-tall weeds growing out of the cracks.

Vinny blessed his love of walking and clear liquor for keeping his figure trim and svelte. He slid in between the easement and worked his way back to the house he targeted.

The dog waited in the backyard. She was a pretty little Cocker Spaniel with bright golden fur, almost like a King Charles, and the expressive, playful eyes for which the breed was known. She heard the strange human approach and rose from her feet to cock her head at him.

Cocker head at him. Heh.

“Hey, sweetheart,” he said with a smile, pulling the bolt cutters from his pocket. “Boy, you’re a beauty. And so small, too. You can't weigh more than what, twenty pounds? You're going to make one of those boys a tasty snack. Speaking of a tasty snack."

He paused his work of cutting the links on the fence and pulled a bacon treat from his pocket. That stuff was like candy to dogs, and this one was no exception. It perked its ears up—well, as “up” as a Cocker Spaniel could get its ears—and tentatively approached Vinny.

Vinny looked up at the doghouse in one corner of the yard. The dog’s name was written in bold letters across the top. He grinned and said, “Here, Macy. Come here, girl. You want a treat?”

Macy cocked her head again, confused. How did this human know her name?

He held the treat up and called, “You want some bacon, Macy?”

Macy perked up again and trotted close. This was a nice human, like the kids she ran into at the dog park sometime. He only wanted to give Macy a treat and scratch her behind her ears and tell her she was a good girl. That was all right.

He tossed the treat to her, and she caught it in the air, then barked proudly. Vinny grinned and pulled out another treat. “You can have this one when I get inside,” he said.

A few more snips took care of the fence, and Vinny gave Macy the promised treat. He put his bolt cutter away and set his bag on the ground. Macy was a small dog, maybe twenty pounds or so. It wouldn't take much of a dose to knock her out. Half a pill should do.

Vinny carefully opened one of the white pills and emptied half of the powder onto a small slip of rolling paper. It had been nearly fifteen years since his last cigarette—not a fan of cancer, was Vincent Mariano—but the supplies, the paraphernalia, the police called it, were of great use to him in his work.

He reached into his bag for the last treat, a peanut butter flavored cupcake that had proven to be a favorite of all dogs from teacup to titan. He carefully spooned a hole out of the center of the cupcake and dropped in the powder, then tamped the peanut butter back over the top of it.

"All right, Macy," he said, "Here's a nice, delicious—"

He stopped when his eyes fell on a pair of black boots. He looked up and saw that the owner of the boots wore a black ski mask as well. Black gloves, a black t-shirt, and a black mask that looked like a wolf.

And a black shock collar in his right hand.

"Shit," Vinny said.

He managed to get halfway to his feet before the stranger clamped the shock collar around his neck.

"Hey!" Vinny cried, "What the—"

His words were choked short by a jolt of electricity that clamped his teeth together and stiffened him like a pole. He shuddered as fifty thousand volts robbed him of control of his body. The electricity cut short, and he fell to the ground, gasping and jerking as spasms wracked him.

"What…" he choked. "What…"

Electricity coursed through him again, and his teeth clamped shut once more. He tasted blood and realized he had bitten through his tongue.

The electricity cut out again, and a muffled voice said, "Where?"

"What?" Vinny coughed. "Where what?"

The stranger lifted a small remote and calmly adjusted a setting.

"Hey, wait," Vinny said, "Please…"

His pleas were drowned out by another jolt of current, this one noticeably more powerful than the first two. When the shock cut out again, Vinny felt his heart stumble a few beats before grudgingly resuming its rhythm.

This was very bad.

"Where?" the stranger repeated.

Vinny thought hard. What could anyone possibly want to know from him? It had to be something to do with the gang. If they knew Vinnie, that meant it had to do with the dogfighting ring.

So where what?

The stranger lifted the remote again, and Vinny forgot all about thought, forgot all about anything but saving his own life. "They keep the dogs in an old warehouse on Jackson Street! The fights happen all over the place, backyards usually. They just hire me to pick up the dogs. I don't train 'em, I don't fight 'em."

The stranger nodded. "Thank you."

He adjusted the setting on the collar again, twisting a dial clockwise until Vinny heard a click.

"Oh man," he whined. "I'm just trying to make a living man."

Those were the last words Vincent Mariano ever spoke. The man pressed a button, and a surge of liquid heat poured from the collar into Vinny's brain. His eyes rolled back in his sockets, and his teeth clattered like a wind-up toy. His arms and legs drummed the ground, and a burning sensation filled his nostrils as the skin on his neck melted.

The collar stopped, and so did Vinny's heart. His head lolled over to the right, and the last thing he was aware of was Macy trotting happily back to her doghouse, the cupcake in her mouth.

CHAPTER ONE

"Hey, Bold," Decker called. "Ten bucks says I get Gutierrez to sleep with me by the end of the week."

Faith scoffed. "Make it a hundred. Your sorry ass couldn't convince Garth to sleep with you."

Garth, a six-foot-four, two-hundred-eighty pound behemoth who liked firing his M249 from the hip and had once bent a length of rebar into a pretzel in Faith's presence, leered at Decker.

"Hell, I ain't proud," Decker said, "Be gentle with me, Daddy, and I'll do whatever you want me to do."

They all laughed at that, and Garth said, "Fortunately for you, I'm worn out after spending the night with your wife, so you get a pass."

The banter continued, one of the few constants in Kajran, along with long, uninterrupted stretches of mind-numbing boredom, something the banter often relieved, and the occasional roadside bomb, something no one acknowledged and everyone thought about.

They had been fortunate enough to avoid the roadside bombs on the three-hour journey from Gadamsa. The Taliban had been unusually quiet recently, probably dealing with the resurgent offensive toward Mazar-i-Sharif in the North, that—if successful, when *successful—would cut them off from Russian support.*

How funny that less than forty years ago, they had fought the Russians, but now that the U.S. was the foreign power, they were right in bed with them. Probably the same people that strategized how to kill Afghani people was now planning ways to use them to kill Americans.

Not that there was anything Faith could do about that. Those decisions were so far above her pay grade she would have to pay someone to be allowed to look at the building where those decisions were made.

So she just picked up her rifle, cracked crude jokes with her brothers and sisters, and waited for them to call her number and send her back home.

"Well, what about you then, Bold?" Decker called with a grin, "You want some help keeping warm tonight?"

Faith smiled sweetly at him and said, "Thanks, but I prefer men."

The others howled laughter. Decker widened his grin and offered Faith a finger. She kept her smile on him a moment longer before turning to face forward. The drab two-story concrete wall of Camp Ghost rose a half-mile distant. Faith relaxed a little. The risk of bombs was gone. The Taliban couldn't get within a mile of the base without being picked off by the long-range snipers posted at each corner. They were home safe again.

She glanced back at Decker, who grinned and winked at her. She rolled her eyes and shook her head but kept her smile.

Decker was cute. He wasn't remotely her type of personality, but he was good-looking enough. Maybe she could use a little help keeping warm.

"You know him?"

Faith looked up from the pictures at Desrouleaux and nodded. "Yeah. Knew him anyway. I hadn't seen him in over eleven years, but I know him. That's Corporal Decker."

"Staff Sergeant Decker," Desrouleaux said, "but yeah, that's him. You two serve together?"

"Yes," she said, "briefly. When did he die?"

"Coroner says night before last. Looks like he was hit before he could put up a fight."

"That makes sense," Faith said, "Decker wasn't the kind of man you fought fair. He was the unit's boxing champion. That means something in the Corps."

"No doubt," Desrouleaux said. He sighed and slumped in his chair. "So why did West go after him? Just to mess with you?"

Faith felt a stab of guilt. "Yes," she said reluctantly. "I think so."

"Christ." Desrouleaux shook his head. "Why you? Just because Trammell couldn't kill you?"

"I guess so," Faith said, shifting uncomfortably. "Look, you know he was in California. Have you tried retracing his steps? If we find out where he came from, maybe we can have an idea where he's going?"

"We're working on it," Desrouleaux said. "So that's all this guy was to you? Just someone you served with?"

Faith knew that Desrouleaux needed to ask her these questions. She wasn't allowed to work on the Copycat Killer case, but she was a person of interest right now since his latest victim was someone known to Faith, and it was now known to the FBI that West was motivated—at least recently—by a desire to torment Faith.

Still, Faith felt like a criminal under a microscope while the seasoned detective worked steadily to break her down and elicit some terrible secret.

"That's all," she said. She didn't think it important for Desrouleaux to know about the brief romantic fling they'd had in Kajran.

"So how did West know? Did you guys talk about your military service?"

"So what was serving in the Corps like?"

Faith chuckled and shook her head. "That's kind of like asking what it's like being in the FBI."

West shrugged. "Well? What was it like?"

She shook her head again. "Um... God, where do I start?" It was an honest question. Any answer she could think of seemed as reductive as the question. Finally, she settled on, "Well, it was fun while it lasted."

"Why?" he asked, not noting the sarcasm in her voice, or else noting it and choosing to ignore it.

She shifted in her seat, not sure why she was suddenly so uncomfortable. "Well... I mean, there's a lot to unpack there."

"Unpack some of it," West insisted. "There's no rush. We don't even need to start with anything particularly important. I'm just trying to get a sense of who you are, and to know that, I need to get a sense of who you were."

Faith hesitated while she tried to think of something to say. She didn't want to talk about combat. That wasn't a subject she looked forward to broaching with a psychologist. The rest of it was mostly stuff that civilians wouldn't understand, private jokes and unique experiences that would make no sense to anyone who wasn't in the Corps.

So what could she tell him that would satisfy his curiosity but not risk sparking a conversation she wasn't ready for?

"Well," she said, "I hooked up with one of the guys in my unit, and our platoon sergeant caught us."

He blinked, clearly not expecting that kind of revelation. Faith was nearly as surprised as he was. What did it say about her that she decided to avoid a personal conversation by telling West about the time her platoon sergeant caught her having sex?

Maybe that was a question for another session.

"Really," Dr. West said. "That sounds... interesting."

She chuckled. "Do I win the most shocking revelation award?"

"Oh, you'd be surprised the things people tell me," Dr. West replied, "but that is definitely not what I thought you'd say."

"What did you think I'd say?"

"I thought you would comment on the brotherhood you felt for your fellow Marines and what an honor it was to follow them into battle."

"A Marine doesn't need to say that out loud," she replied, "It's understood."

"Of course," Dr. West said. "When people go into war together, there is a bond there that can never be severed."

A stab of guilt shot through Faith. When was the last time she had talked to anyone from Dog Company? She hadn't even gone to the five-year reunion.

"Of course," she said, keeping her voice neutral.

"So tell me about this boy," he said, "or this man, I apologize."

She smiled slightly, "No, boy, just about sums it up. He was the stereotypical bad boy with a baby face. Movie star smile, nice arms, blue eyes. Not much of a lover, but you took whatever you could get over there."

So much for avoiding personal conversations.

"Did this boy have a name?"

She furrowed her eyes. "Well, yeah, but why do you want to know?"

"Well, you were intimate with him. He must be important to you."

She laughed. "Decker? No, he was never important. I wasn't important to him, either, though. We were just young and horny and available. That's really all it came down to. And since the platoon sergeant walked in on us, it never happened again."

"Well, this Decker was *important to you, Faith, even if you don't realize it," West insisted. "You were intimate with him, and even if it seemed to you like it was only scratching an itch, it was certainly far more than that. You chose to reach out for human contact, and when you did, you chose Decker."*

"So why him?"

Faith blinked and looked back at Desrouleaux. "Why, who?"

Desrouleaux glanced at his partner, a young agent named Chavez, who stood nervously, unsure what to do. Faith was the most well-known and respected agent in the Philadelphia Field Office, and Chavez was barely out of her training uniform. She still raised her hand to speak in meetings.

Faith spared her the need to interrogate a senior agent. “I don’t know. Best guess, he just recalled me mentioning the name once and decided to hunt him down.”

“How many other names do you think you mentioned to him?” Desrouleaux asked.

The corners of Faith’s lips turned down. For a while, West was the only person Faith really talked to. She had shared a lot of names with him, far too many to recall.

But she had to recall them. “I don’t know off the top of my head,” she said, “but a lot.”

Desrouleaux sighed. “Dammit.”

“Yeah,” she said,” I know.”

“Do you think you could come up with a list?” he asked. “Of any name you can remember telling him and what their relationship is to you? I don’t know how it would matter how closely they’re related since his first choice was a guy you hadn’t talked to in over a decade. Was he an old boyfriend or something?”

“No, not a boyfriend,” Faith replied. Which was perfectly true.

Desrouleaux shook his head and scratched his chin. “Well, we’ll file it all away with the rest. Sorry about this, Faith.”

Faith managed a half smile that disappeared the moment the door closed.

So West hadn’t been in Philadelphia after all. He had gone as far away from the Atlantic Coast as he could. Now James Decker was dead. He probably hadn't thought about her in years, and now he was dead just because West knew that he had once known her.

When Franklin West, ostensibly a psychologist, in reality the Copycat Killer whose murders far outstripped those of the original Donkey Killer, killed her friend and mentor Gordon Clark, he left her a note that explicitly threatened her boyfriend, David Friedman, her partner, Special Agent Michael Prince and his fiancée, Ellie West, who turned out to be the ex-wife of none other than Franklin West.

Ellie Prince now. They had married. She hadn't been invited to the wedding, primarily because, as part of her obsession with finding the Copycat Killer, she had interpreted Turk’s initial dislike of Ellie as evidence that Ellie was the Copycat Killer herself.

She was certain that West would be here in Philadelphia and that his next move would be against David. Instead, he—likely anticipating her thought process—had traveled across the country and murdered a man she hadn’t thought of in years.

Except for ten minutes in West's office.

He knew that Decker wasn't important to her. She told him he was just the other party in a funny memory and nothing more. There were dozens of more important names she had given him.

And maybe he would go after one of them next.

She left the office and headed home, feeling everyone's eyes boring into her back. Since being reinstated a few weeks ago, Faith had felt like an outsider. People she'd worked with for years avoided her in the hallway. Everyone treated her like a bomb waiting to go off, and the fact that she had earned that reputation didn't make it feel any better.

And now this. Death followed Faith like a cloud, and if not for Turk's enthusiastic greeting when she walked inside, she might have spent a sleepless night staring moodily at her blank tv screen.

But how could you not smile when an eighty-pound puppy jumped into your arms and started exuberantly licking your face?

"Hey, boy," she said. "Sorry, I'm home late. I had to talk to Desrouleaux. You remember him? Short, dyed hair, smells like maple donuts?"

Turk barked, and Faith laughed. "Well, he… he just needed to talk to me." She wasn't ready to talk about it, not even to Turk.

"Let's eat some dinner, huh?" she said. "Then we'll watch that movie you like about the dog who rescues all those kids."

Turk barked exuberantly, and Faith headed to the kitchen. An hour later, she sat on the couch, Turk in front of her, his tail switching back and forth with excitement as a Saint Bernard carefully navigated his way down a snow-covered slope to help a crying toddler. When the dog slipped, Turk, who had seen this movie at least fifty times before and knew that the dog would regain his balance and successfully rescue the last child, barked and whined anxiously. When the dog deposited the child safely into the arms of her waiting mother, Turk leaped and barked and howled for joy.

Faith smiled as she watched him. He turned to her, panting and smiling, and she saw the chipped tooth on his left side.

Her smile faded slightly. West had tried to take Turk from her, too, but Turk had escaped and left West a little present on his way out the door.

"He's not getting you," she said. "Nope. Not you, boy."

Turk wasn't sure why Faith was suddenly serious, but he barked in solidarity and turned back to the movie, where the Saint Bernard was proudly accepting a medal for bravery from the Governor of Colorado.

After the movie, Faith put Turk to bed. He closed his eyes and fell asleep almost immediately, a skill he had no doubt learned from the Marine Corps. Faith herself had shared that skill up until two years ago. Jethro Trammell had seen to it that she rarely slept without nightmares, and sleep was no longer so easily attained.

Nor would tonight be any different. West may have been a stand-in for Trammell in Faith's psyche at first, but he was the big Evil now. Trammell was dead and gone, West was still active. He had killed one of Faith's friends and one of Faith's former comrades, and she had no doubt he wouldn't stop there.

So, she thought back to her many sessions with West, to the names, both important and unimportant, that she had told him, and began to write. She had no idea if there was any rhyme or reason to Faith's choices. Decker was a fond memory of hers but not a particularly important one.

He's spreading us thin, she thought. *He's trying to overwork us and find cracks in the armor.*

She knew this was true, but she had no choice. He would keep killing until he got what he wanted or until he was caught. At the moment, they weren't anywhere near catching him, so he would keep killing.

Just like a chess master, he had forced Faith and the Bureau into a corner. They had no choice but to play his game right now and hope he made a mistake.

Before they made a mistake.

CHAPTER TWO

Gina Sawyer hummed a tune to herself as she sliced the potatoes. The Hollingsworths were coming over for dinner, and she was making ribeye steaks with garlic mashed potatoes and roasted green beans.

Gina was not—as so many at the school district insisted—attracted to Jeff Hollingsworth. He really was just a friend, and anyway, his wife, Laura, was the sweetest creature alive. Besides, she was in love with her husband. It really was amazing the kind of stories people made up.

The doorbell rang, and she yelped in surprise. Was that them already? Goodness, she had said five o'clock! It was barely three! Maybe Henry had ordered a package?

She rinsed her hands and wiped them on the kitchen towel, then headed for the door. She looked through the peephole and saw two men in black suits with sunglasses on. She gasped slightly, and when she looked behind them and saw the navy-blue van with the words FBI emblazoned on the side, she gasped again.

She opened the door a crack and said, "Um… hello? Can I help you?"

"Gina Burgess?" the man to the left asked in a humorless voice.

"Um… it's Sawyer now," she said, "Burgess is my maiden name. Is this… what is this?"

"I'm Special Agent Heath Dawson," the man said, "this is my partner, Special Agent Garrett Edgely. May we speak with you for a few moments?"

"Um… I'm sorry." Gina took a step back and shook her head in confusion. "What is going on? Why is the FBI at my house?"

"Do you remember a Faith Bold, ma'am?"

"Faith Bold…" Gina's eyes widened. "From high school?"

"Yes, ma'am. You two were lab partners in freshman chemistry."

"Faith Bold from high school," Fina repeated incredulously. "Why are you two here to talk to me about Faith Bold from freshman chemistry?"

"May we come inside?" Dawson asked.

"I mean…" Gina hesitated, "am I in trouble?"

Dawson and Edgely shared a look. “I think it would be best if we had this conversation inside, ma’am,” Dawson said.

Gina’s heart pounded. What the hell was going on? Faith *Bold?* “Well… do I need a lawyer?”

“No, ma’am,” Dawson said, “To be clear, you are not in any legal trouble, nor are you suspected of any criminal activity. However, we have a matter of a very sensitive nature that we must discuss with you.”

Gina’s heart continued to pound. If she wasn’t in trouble, then why was the FBI here? “Um… sure,” she said, “Come inside.”

She stepped back and allowed the two agents to enter. Their eyes immediately scanned the décor and the furnishings, observing everything and cataloguing it. Gina felt like a bug under a microscope.

“Can I offer you something to drink?” she asked.

"No, thank you," Dawson said.

Edgely shook his head.

“Okay,” she said, “Um, well, I suppose we can sit in the living room.”

“Thank you, ma’am,” Dawson replied.

Gina thought about telling him to call her by her first name, but somehow the thought of that robotic voice uttering her name was even worse than being called ma’am.

The two agents sat, their postures as stiff as their expressions. Gina remained standing, arms folded protectively over her chest.

“Ma’am,” Dawson began, “there’s no easy way to say this, so I’m just going to be direct. We believe you may be targeted by a serial killer.”

When Gina was eleven years old, her cousin had died after falling down an open manhole cover that the city had neglected to cordon off or cover. Gina remembered finding her parents crying on the couch and hearing them tell her that Cousin Georgie had passed into Heaven. The first words out of her mouth were, “But I just talked to him this morning.”

She spent the rest of that week in a fog, unable to understand how Georgie could have been laughing and joking with her that morning and be dead that afternoon. It didn’t make sense. It felt like she had stepped into a dream from which she couldn’t wake up.

She felt the same fog now as she processed the agent’s words. Her legs felt suddenly numb, and she sat slowly and tried to wrap her head around everything.

“Um,” she said, “I… what?”

She hated that that was all she could think of to say, but her mind kept hitching back to those words like an old record player skipping over the last portion of the song.

Serial killer. Serial killer. Serial killer.

Dawson and Edgely glanced at each other. "Are you familiar with the Copycat Donkey Killer case?" Dawson asked.

Gina shook her head and unconsciously began chewing on her fingernails, a habit that, ironically, had ended the year she had started high school, the year she had met Faith Bold.

"Um," she said, "the guy who cuts people to pieces in Philadelphia?"

The agents shared another look. "More or less," Dawson demurred.

"Well, it's not more or less, it's what he does," Gina said with a touch of exasperation. Her senses were returning to her, but that was proving to be little comfort.

Dawson nodded. "Well, we believe that he's targeting a number of past and present associates of Faith Bold."

"Why?" Gina asked.

"We're not at liberty to say."

Gina stared at him. "You're telling me that a brutal serial killer is threatening my life because of a woman I haven't seen in over fifteen years, and you can't tell me why?"

"That's correct. I'm sorry, ma'am."

"Sorry? You're sure—" Gina bit her fingernails again and looked out the window. Yolanda Ramirez was working in her garden, carefully tending to the hydrangeas and poppies and chrysanthemums she had arranged in a long, narrow planter her husband Diego had built for her a few years ago. She looked through the window at Gina and smiled.

Gina lifted her fingers in a brief wave, then pressed them to her lips again. "So… why are you telling me then?" she asked.

"The Bureau is willing to place you and your husband under surveillance until the killer has been arrested," Dawson said. " We would station agents outside your home to watch for any suspicious activity.

Gina felt that fog settles over her again. "So, basically, you'd wait for this killer to show up and hope you get to him before he gets to me.

"Yes, ma'am."

"How would I recognize that it's you? I mean, how would I tell that your agents are the ones watching me and not the killer? If someone comes to the door and says they're FBI, how do I know they're telling the truth?"

"We don't anticipate the agents will need to speak with you. In the event they do, they will come to you in pairs, just as Agent Edgely and I have. We believe this killer is working alone. If an individual comes to you alone claiming to be FBI, you can reasonably assume they're not telling the truth."

"You *believe* he's working alone?"

"Yes, ma'am."

A point behind Gina's left eye began to throb. "When would… I mean… When would all of this happen?"

"Immediately."

Gina released a noise somewhere between a gasp, a laugh and a sob. "So, just to make sure I have everything straight, you're offering to put my husband and I under guard because I am in danger of being murdered by a serial killer because I once built a volcano out of papier mache, baking soda and vinegar with Faith Bold in freshman year of high school, and you can't tell me why that is. Is Faith Bold the Copycat Killer?"

"No, ma'am," Dawson replied.

"Stop calling me ma'am!" she snapped.

"I apologize, Mrs. Sawyer."

Gina stood and crossed the living room again. Her mind screamed at her to just take the deal, to do whatever she needed to do to be safe, but an irrational part of her brain insisted that if she did that, then she would somehow be putting herself in more danger, as though by admitting to the existence of that danger she made herself vulnerable to it."

"So you'd just watch us from across the street or something."

Dawson and Edgely shared a look again. Gina had to quell an irrationally powerful surge of anger.

Stop treating me with kid gloves! Goddammit, I don't have cancer!

A second thought echoed that one, a vaguely taunting thought, as though her own mind were reveling in the destruction of her sense of safety. *No, you don't have cancer. You have a target on your forehead.*

"No.," Dawson said. "We would also place video and audio recording devices around your house and station two agents to monitor your home and your activities."

"Does surveillance include protection? Like bodyguards?"

Dawson and Edgely shared another look, and if Gina had to see that look again, she would tear her own eyes out. "No, ma'am," Dawson said, "we would respond immediately if the killer was sighted, but we wouldn't provide personal protection."

"So I'm only safe as long as I remain in my own home where your agents can see me?"

Dawson and Edgely started to turn toward each other, and Gina couldn't hold back her anger. "Just answer the damned question!"

Dawson sighed. "To the best of our knowledge, the killer only targets people when they're alone. If you make sure that you leave your house only in daylight and in the company of others, you should be safe."

There it was again. "To the best of our knowledge." "You should be safe."

Gina folded her arms across her chest again. She looked around at her home, so small and quaint and quiet and *safe*. This was a *safe* neighborhood, dammit. How could she suddenly be targeted by a murderer?

"Can I have some time to think about it?" she asked.

"We can give you until nine o'clock this evening," Dawson said, "I'm afraid that's the best we can do. We have other people to visit."

Gina sighed and turned toward the kitchen. Her freshly peeled and sliced potatoes were slowly browning from the exposure to the air.

"I'll leave my card on the table," Dawson said. "If you decide to accept our offer, please let me know."

The two agents left her then, standing with her arms crossed and her fingers pressed to her lips. Gina tried to remember Faith, and couldn't come up with anything other than braces, blue eyes and pigtails. The two of them were friendly, but they weren't exactly friends.

And yet, that was enough to put her in the crosshairs of a psycho.

CHAPTER THREE

Faith left the shower, a towel wrapped around her waist. She walked into the living room, and David's eyes widened. He looked her up and down appreciatively and said, "Wow. Getting back with you was a good idea."

Faith giggled and said, "Why do you say that?"

She turned and let the towel fall as she did. David caught her halfway to the kitchen and decided to show his answer rather than speak it.

After, they sat together on the couch, Faith's head on his chest, his arm around her shoulders. The past three weeks had pretty much been endless sex and cuddling, which made it feel exactly like what it was intended to be: a fresh start for the two of them.

And it had been wonderful right up until the week before when Faith had learned of Decker's murder and West's presumed decision to target everyone she had ever mentioned during their sessions. Now, Faith worried that once more, David was in danger.

She hadn't told him yet. The last time she had asked him to leave town, he had done so, but the stress of leaving his patients for several weeks had prompted their earlier separation.

But it was selfish not to tell him. She couldn't allow him to remain in danger. The past several nights she had barely slept for fear that she would wake to a phone call from the Bureau telling her that David had been found cut apart just like all of West's victims.

She pushed herself to an upright position. David looked questioningly at her, and when he saw her expression, she noticed tension come to his face. It hurt to see because she knew it meant he was going to resist what she had to say.

"I have to tell you something," she said.

"All right," he replied cautiously.

She took a deep breath and said, "West killed someone else."

"I'm sorry to hear that," David replied. "Someone you knew?"

"Someone I used to know," she said. "Not for a long time, but I did know him."

"I see," he said noncommittally. "I'm sorry."

"It's okay," she said, "I'm fine. Like I said, I hadn't known him in a long time, but… I know you."

His lips thinned, and Faith could tell he knew what was coming. "You think he's after me again?"

"I don't know for sure that he ever stopped being after you," she said. "I think he might have just been forced away because of the investigation. What I do know is that he's killing again, and he still seems interested in people connected to me."

"So this person he killed," David said, "how close were the two of you?"

"Not particularly. We just served together in the war for a few months."

Skepticism came into David's eyes and voice. "Okay. And you're sure that he was targeted because of you? This isn't just one of West's random killings?"

"No," she said, "it's definitely not random."

"Where was this killing?" he asked. "Here, in Philadelphia?"

"No," she said, "it was in California, a place called Lucerne Valley."

He sighed and said, "Well, I'm very sorry, Faith, and I'm not trying to belittle your feelings or the fact that a man is dead, but are you really sure that it has anything to do with you?"

She blinked. "Well, yeah. Why else would West target him?"

"That's what I'm trying to say," David replied. "Maybe he didn't target him. Maybe he's just in hiding in California, and he attacked someone opportunistically. Maybe it didn't have anything to do with you at all. You said you only knew this guy for a few months in the Marines, right?"

"Yeah, but West *did* target him."

"But why does that have something to do with you? If he was targeting people close to you, then he would come after me or Michael."

"That's what I'm saying," Faith insisted, "I'm afraid he will come after you."

"But why kill someone you barely knew first? You've known lots of people, Faith. Maybe you just happened to know this victim."

"No," she said, "I… I mentioned him to West in a session."

David lifted an eyebrow. "So he *was* important to you."

“No!” Faith insisted more sharply than she intended. His insistence reminded her of West’s own words to her when she spoke of Decker. “He just came up. A lot of people just came up.”

"So why put himself at risk just in the hope that a random past association with someone might cause you guilt? Why allow yourself to feel guilt?”

“I didn’t say I was guilty,” she replied, “I just worry about you.”

“Well, don’t,” he said, a little testily, probably because he knew what was coming. “We’ve been through this before, Faith. I really don’t want to go through it again, not after we’ve agreed to start over.”

Faith’s heart broke, but it would break further if David was hurt. “I know, but this is different. He’s actually killing people close to me now.”

“So he *was* close to you.”

“No, I…” Faith felt herself getting angry, but she knew it wouldn’t help to allow her emotions to rule her now. She took a breath to steady herself and said, “I don’t know exactly what West is thinking beyond that he wants to hurt me.”

That wasn’t precisely true, but Faith didn’t want to get into an in-depth explanation of West’s motives right now. “I’m just saying, since he is active again, the FBI is offering surveillance to anyone close to me, and—David, please just listen!”

David had stood in the middle of that sentence and placed his hands on the back of his head. He paced around the living room, shaking his head. “Faith, I can’t keep having this argument with you. I can’t leave Philadelphia again.”

“But—”

“Faith, no,” he said sharply. He softened his voice and sighed. “Look, he’s on the other side of the country right now. What’s he going to do, come back here to Philadelphia where there are several different federal and local agencies hunting for him, and try to kill me just to hurt you?”

“Yes,” Faith said, “absolutely he will. Maybe not tomorrow or next week, but one day.”

“Well, the one-day part is the part that’s frustrating, Faith. I can’t just leave indefinitely and wait for you to tell me that everything’s safe again. I almost lost my practice the last time.”

“You’ll definitely lose your practice if you’re dead,” she pointed out.

“Faith, the answer’s no,” he said in exasperation.

"So you're just going to stick around and wait for him to find you?"

"I'm going to live my life without fear," he replied. "Plenty of people die every day. Some of them are even murdered. Most of them aren't targets of anything. They're just in the wrong place at the wrong time."

"Exactly," Faith said, "the wrong place."

"That's not my point."

"No," Faith said, fear turning to anger and adding belligerence to her voice. "Your point is that you should just wait around for a man who has explicitly threatened to murder you to do exactly as he promised he would, and I should just, what… wait for it to happen?"

"I'm not going to argue with you about this," he said, grabbing his clothes and starting to dress. "Faith, I accepted when I started dating you—both times—that being in love with an FBI agent meant there was a possibility I would lose you to violence. You don't think I worry every time you go out there in the field? You don't think it keeps me up at night knowing you do things like split up from your partner to chase a serial killer in an underground mine that's unmapped and unstable? You don't think that scares me? You don't think it pisses me off to know how little you value your own life at times?"

Faith lowered her eyes. She didn't have an answer for him.

"I'm not going to tell you to quit your job, Faith," David continued. "I want to." She lifted her eyes to him in surprise. "Yeah," he affirmed. "I want you to quit sometimes. I hate that I'll always be second place to your job—" she began to protest, and he held up his hand "—I accept that your job has to come first, and I'm not asking you to change. I'm only saying that I wish sometimes that you weren't in the FBI out risking your life regularly hunting psychotic and dangerous men.

"But you are, and you'll keep doing it. If I asked you to stop now, if I told you to quit your job or I would break up with you, would you?"

She lowered her eyes again and softly said, "No."

"No," he repeated, "and I wouldn't ask you to because I know how important your work is to you. Well, my work is important to me, Faith. Just because I'm not out rescuing people and hunting bad guys doesn't mean that I don't value what I do. Every job carries risk. Every *life* carries risk. But I think even you would agree that your job—your life—carries more risk than mine."

Faith hated that argument. She hated that it was true. At any given moment, Faith was in more danger than David was.

And while David might never have asked her to change, several others had. Michael, in particular, had been very vocal about his disapproval of her tendency to ignore or dismiss risk in her pursuit of killers. She wouldn't change, even knowing that he was right.

But she wished like hell that David would just do as she asked. Didn't he know how much more important his life was to Faith than her own life?

Well, she couldn't exactly tell him *that*, could she?

Her phone rang. Michael. She looked up at David, and he nodded. "It's okay," he said softly. "Take it." He smiled sadly. "Knowing that you can get called away at any moment is another thing I have to accept."

She offered the ghost of a smile in return and answered. "Hello?"

"Well, you sound just overjoyed to hear my voice," Michael said drily.

"You seem equally excited to call," she replied just as drily.

"Story of my life," he said. "We have another case. Boss wants us in the office within the hour. I plan to be there in exactly fifty-nine minutes, which leaves me enough time to stop for coffee at the Morning Glory. If you want, you can meet me there. Otherwise, I'll see you in the office."

"I'll meet you there," she said. "I could use some coffee."

"Works for me. See you soon."

She hung up and said, "Before I leave, David, I want you to know that I understand what you're saying—"

"Let's leave it at that," he interrupted, not unkindly.

She lowered her gaze and nodded.

CHAPTER FOUR

"You look even more excited to see me than to talk to me," Michael said when Faith arrived at the coffee shop.

She sighed. "I just wish we could meet for reasons other than the brutal deaths of innocents."

"Well, Wal-Mart's hiring," he said, "from what I understand, the job of greeter is marginally less traumatizing than the job of Special Agent."

Faith chuckled. "I'd be fired within a week for chasing someone down over a shoplifted candy bar."

"That's your problem," he said, "I will have no problem looking the other way and letting the twenty-year-old security agent tackle them."

She grinned at him. "Feeling our age a little bit, are we?"

Michael was five months away from his fortieth birthday and had made no secret of his displeasure about that fact. "I've been feeling my age since I was twenty-five," he replied. "It just gets worse and worse every year."

"Well, maybe you'll get to do Gordon's job soon," Faith suggested. "Then you can sit behind a desk and listen to all the agents grouse about funding and authority in the field."

He chuckled without humor. "I won't be SSA as long as you're my partner." Faith's smile faded, and he clarified, "Joking, Faith. That was a joke. If I wanted to be SSA, I would have applied. Desrouleaux turned it down, too, and no one else is qualified. It's just the Boss for now."

They got in line for coffee, and Faith asked, "How long do you think the Boss has?"

"'Til what?"

"Until he retires?"

He smiled wryly at her. "Why are you gunning for the job?"

She laughed aloud at that, "Me? Hell no. Even if someone in Washington got stupid and offered me the job, I wouldn't want it. Me as a bureaucrat? No, thank you."

"I think you'd be a good SAC," Michael said.

She stared frankly at him, and he chuckled. "Okay, I was just being polite."

"Don't bother," she said, "I know what my limits are. Maybe I'll train one day. Even I'll have to admit to being too old to keep wrestling mutants in caves eventually."

"You'd be a good trainer," Michael offered. "No joke. You're a damned good detective, and even if you can't train that, you're also a damned good K9 handler. Firearms need a little work, but if you had nothing to do but practice—"

She shoved him playfully and said, "Well, I have a while before I have to worry about that, at least."

They reached the front of the line and placed their orders: coffee for Faith—"black like your soul," Michael joked—and a doppio macchiato—a "dopey Mac," Faith retorted with a grin—for Michael. They received their coffees and sat at a table near the back of the café where they could keep an eye on the front door and the bathroom doors. Faith wondered when that instinct developed in law enforcement to always have eyes on the entrances and exits. It wasn't something she had been taught. It was just something she did now.

"Desrouleaux and Chavez talked to Ellie yesterday," Michael said.

"Oh yeah?" Faith replied. "How'd she take it?"

When Faith gave Desrouleaux the list of names mentioned in her sessions with West, he had decided to petition for the FBI to offer surveillance to every potential victim. Since the people in question were in danger due indirectly to their association with an active-duty agent, they had agreed readily. Now, agents across the country were breaking the news to everyone Faith had known since high school. None of them had sent angry and panicked letters or emails to Faith yet, but she was pretty sure that once someone figured out her contact info, she would get a lot of hate from people whose entire lives had suddenly been upended.

More fun to look forward to.

"Not so well," Michael replied, answering Faith's question. "She made it clear that she was staying put."

The look on Michael's face suggested she had said more than just that. "Was that all?" she prompted.

He sighed. "Well, she offered some suggestions. Most of them had to do with relieving you of duty. A few had to do with shooting West on sight."

"I like that one," Faith said. "She has my full support there."

He chuckled briefly, then said, "They offered her surveillance."

Faith hadn't mentioned the surveillance to David, and she didn't plan to. If he wouldn't take himself somewhere safe, then maybe she could force at least a little safety on him. "Which one did she choose?"

"Neither," Michael replied. "She said that she was staying put, and if she saw a damned FBI van outside of her house, she'd report the Bureau for harassment."

"Wow," Faith said, "I'm surprised to hear that."

"I'm not," Michael said grouchily. "She was married to that schmuck for twelve years, took two years to divorce him, and now her first year of true separation from him has been dominated by him and their relationship. She's at the point now where I think she'd almost rather die than deal with it anymore."

"What do you think?" Faith asked.

"I told Desrouleaux to watch the house anyway," he said. "I gave him some places where agents could camp out that Ellie wouldn't notice. I would rather she was in the loop on this, but she wouldn't appreciate that. She doesn't want to be constantly reminded of West."

"Hmm," Faith said, sipping her coffee. "Well, David wasn't very happy about it either."

"No?" Michael said, "they talked to him too?"

"I did," she replied. "I asked him to leave, but he wouldn't. I didn't tell him about the surveillance."

"Probably smart," Michael opined. "Keep him as safe as you can." He sighed and added, "It sucks because I understand where Elli's coming from. If I were her, I'd probably feel the same way. But I'm *not* her, and I understand a lot more about this than she does. I just wish I could let her read my thoughts for a moment to know why it's so important that they watch her."

"Me too," Faith said.

She smiled at Michael. It was nice to have the two of them on the same page again. "Well, with the Bureau watching them, they should be safe enough. West works alone, after all. A pair of armed agents shouldn't have any trouble with him."

"Yeah," Michael said. "Hope so."

***

Grant Monroe—the Boss, as he was affectionately known to his agents—greeted Faith stiffly when she and Michael entered. Faith returned an equally awkward acknowledgment as she took her seat. Turk barked formally, and earned the closest thing to a respectful greeting the Boss was capable of.

Prior to her and Michael's last case, the Boss had suspended her for continuing to pursue West, and she had essentially blackmailed him into letting her keep her job. He agreed with her reasons for staying—that West would escalate if it looked to him like Faith was giving up—but he still refused to allow her to participate actively in the case.

Now, someone else was dead, and Faith was sure it was to get her attention. She planned to ask Michael's help pursuing him, but she hadn't done so yet, knowing that when she did, it would probably be the end of her career and would put his own career at great risk.

Michael had taken it upon himself to keep Faith updated on the case as much as he could, but now that Faith was acknowledged to be the sun around which West orbited, there was no need. She would be kept abreast of it by necessity.

All of which no doubt only compounded the Boss's frustration.

"The case is in Atlanta," the Boss said without preamble when both were seated. "Two victims so far, both believed to be connected to the same criminal organization."

"Who are the victims?" Faith asked.

"Victim one: Harvey Harris. He went by the name H-Bomb back in the days he was a small-time pusher. He'd moved up in the world by the time of his death. He was running his own crew and insisting that people called him by his first name or by Mr. Harris."

"Guess someone took that the wrong way," Michael quipped.

A glare from the Boss wiped away Michael's smile.

"Victim two," he continued. "Vincent Mariano. Used to be a soldier for the Franco Family in Jersey. He ended up disappearing when Tomasso Franco was arrested and his family broke up. I guess he ended up in Atlanta. Homeowner found him dead in their backyard when they returned home. The backyard fence had been cut. Looks like he was trying to steal from them and ended up dead."

"We know that's not the homeowner?" Michael asked.

"Homeowner has an ironclad alibi. He was at work, and three different security cameras confirmed he was there."

"Got it."

"What *do* we know?" Faith asked.

"I just told you," the Boss replied. "The police are treating these like gangland killings, but the crew Harris was running is associated with the Georgia Syndicate."

Michael whistled. The Georgia Syndicate was a loosely associated crime "family" believed to control over thirty percent of the distribution of cocaine in the United States. They were known to be unusually violent and were believed to be responsible for over fifty murders since their formation in the nineties.

That explained why the FBI was involved. If one of the cartels was in a dispute with the Syndicate, they could be looking at a lot more death soon. It was critical that Faith and Michael solve this case as quickly as possible.

"I assume we're leaving tonight?" Michael asked.

"Unless you have somewhere better to be," the Boss replied.

"Do you want me to answer that?" Michael asked drily.

"I do not," the Boss replied. "I want you to get to the airport ASAP and get to Atlanta. The sooner the better."

"Well, the flight leaves when it leaves, doesn't it?"

The Boss glared at him. "You decide to be an extra pain in my ass today, Prince? The plane leaves when the two of you have your butts in seats. So take the damned file and piss off."

He tossed the file at Prince, who caught it with one hand and said, "All right, on our way."

The three of them left the office and headed to the airport. On the way, Michael said, "So what do you think? Gangland killing?"

"Probably," Faith said, "but with the potential to turn into a real problem. Atlanta has its share of street gangs, but they're disorganized and not much of a threat outside of their neighborhoods. The Syndicate likes it that way because there's less infighting, but if there *is* infighting or trouble with rival cartels, they can organize everyone in a heartbeat, and then we're looking at a situation like L.A. in the eighties or New York in the fifties."

"So why us?" Michael asked. "Why not the DEA?"

"I imagine they're involved as much as they can be," Faith opined, "but since drugs aren't considered a primary motivator in this case, they're probably waiting on the outside until we uncover something that gives them an excuse to muscle us out of the way."

"Would I be a bad agent for saying I wouldn't mind being muscled out of the way on this one? There's a reason I steered away from organized crime when I was in training."

“I don’t think it matters,” Faith said. “We’re there to do our jobs and get out. As long as the first part happens, I’m fine with the second one.”

Michael sighed and shook her head. “Between you and me, Faith, I’m no longer ruing the day when it won’t be me having to drop everything in my life to go figure out who killed a couple of scumbags.”

Faith looked over at him and studied his face. The brashness he used to carry was gone, the cockiness mellowed considerably. The lines in his face had deepened, and his eyes showed little of the fire she knew.

This job weighed heavily on everyone. For some, like Faith, the pressure emboldened them, drove them to fight harder and harder until they burned themselves out or finally achieved whatever satisfaction they were looking for.

For others, it wore them down until they were reduced to an echo of who they once were.

Was Michael becoming an echo? Would he, like so many others before him, fade into nothing more than a sad, bitter shell?

And was that any worse than flaming out like a firework the way Faith feared she might?

Go out in a blaze of glory, she used to say to herself. *Don’t fizzle.*

She was nearing her blaze of glory. Michael was fizzling. Only time would tell which of them had made the right choice.

Or if both had made the wrong one.

CHAPTER FIVE

Detective Janet Garvey seemed just as reluctant as Michael to be involved with this case. Her eyes sported dark circles, and her hair didn't look like it had been touched in at least twenty-four hours. She greeted the agents tersely, and her demeanor didn't change as she drove them from an airport to the first crime scene.

"There's not much left there," she warned them. "We have to move quickly whenever we get called to Hansen Street. Your dog bite?"

"If he needs to," Faith replied.

"Good. He might need to. It doesn't happen often, but I know of a few officers who had to be treated for dog bites when the owners 'accidentally' lost control of their animals. Having a dog to protect us might deter some of those accidents."

"Not many PD fans on Hansen Street, huh?" Michael asked.

"No," Garvey said, "that's an understatement."

Faith kept an eye on the scenery passing them by as they navigated through the streets of Atlanta. The buildings near the airport were the typical mix of late-build luxury and old working-class high-rises in varying states of decay and disarray. Past the airport, things settled to a fairly steady progression from well-to-do to middle class to working class and, when they reached downtown, to poor.

Hansen Street was somehow worse. It reminded Faith of Skid Row in Los Angeles, but Skid Row as it had been in the eighties and early nineties before reforms and city projects had worked to (somewhat) clean up the area.

No such projects appeared to have taken place here. The buildings were covered in graffiti, and the street itself was littered with trash. Most of the windows were broken, and the cars that actually ran were old beat-up sedans with mountains of junk visible through the windows.

The locals—as Garvey predicted—were not happy to see law enforcement. They cast stony faces at the officers and made only a token attempt to hide their drugs and their weapons when Garvey put her lights on and led the three agents from the vehicle.

A few of them did have dogs—Rottweilers, Dobermanns, and Pit Bulls. They all growled and barked as the agents passed. Turk bristled but kept his cool otherwise. Recently, the three of them had a case in Arizona where a crazed former vet tech had used chemical pheromones to manipulate a pack of dogs into murdering people. Turk had nearly fallen victim to that chemical and, prior to that, had been cornered by a pack of actual guard dogs while investigating a junkyard.

"Easy boy," Faith said, reaching down to ruffle his fur. "We're okay."

Michael glanced furtively around at the stone-faced locals and said, "Christ, should we have brought backup?"

"Nah," Garvey—the only one among them who was calm—replied. "They're all bark and no bite."

"I thought you said that some of them sicced their dogs on officers before."

"Yes, but we're here investigating the murder of one of their own, you two are feds, and you brought a dog. As long as we don't try to punk anyone, they'll leave us alone."

"I will endeavor not to punk anyone," Michael replied.

Garvey led them into one of the less rundown buildings and into the leasing office. The manager and the security guard present glared at the four of them. "We need the apartment again," she said without introducing the agents. "Feds want to take a look at it."

"What the hell are feds doing here?" the guard asked, glowering at them.

"They're investigating H-Bomb's murder," Garvey replied, "and we need the keys."

"You took all the shit away already," the manager said, "why do you need to go back?"

"Because I said so," Garvey replied shortly, "and you don't want me to follow up on everyone you're renting to who doesn't have a social security number or a credit score."

The manager met Garvey's eyes, her lip curling in contempt. She reached into a drawer and shoved a set of keys at Garvey, who caught them and smiled frostily. "Pleasure doing business with you."

She led the agents out the sliding glass door and into the complex. On their way out, the guard said, "You better keep that dog off my grass."

Faith didn't bother to respond.

The residents gave the agents the same stare those on the street had. Faith decided they would get little help from witnesses, if there were any. This was the kind of neighborhood where people turned up the tv and looked the other way when things happened.

The complex was really just a single building with a rectangular central courtyard. Faith counted thirty units, not including the office and the maintenance room. Considering the size of the building, Faith decided the apartments must be very small.

Garvey led them to a first-floor apartment and opened the door. She led them inside, and Faith was shocked to see the apartment almost bare. There was the ubiquitous sea of trash and dust, but the furniture and appliances were gone. Even the cabinets had been emptied.

Turk started sniffing around to see what he could make of the place. Judging by the emptiness of the place, that was probably their best chance at finding anything useful.

"Christ, how much stuff did you take?" Michael asked.

"Anything illegal or illegally gotten," Garvey replied, "that we knew of, anyway. The rest the neighbors probably took."

That explained why the manager didn't want them in the apartment. "So why are we here? If there's no evidence left, why not just take us to the station."

"I wanted you to get a sense of the neighborhood," Garvey replied, "and I thought it might be helpful to see the apartment while looking at the photos of the evidence. You get a better understanding of things that way."

Faith had to admit she had a point.

"Speaking of," Garvey continued, "Here are the photos. I made copies for each of you."

She handed a small stack of photos to each agent. Faith looked at the first one, and her eyes widened. There was furniture in this picture, but it was all overturned. Blood spatter could be seen all over the room, as though their victim had pirouetted as he was bleeding out.

Harvey Harris had been found on the couch, the only piece of furniture not overturned. He sat slumped forward, his forearms resting on his thighs, his chin planted on his chest. Blood seeped from wounds on his abdomen and shoulders.

"Looks like he put up a fight," Michael said.

"Oh yeah. We believe it took the killer some time to subdue him."

"This seems silly to ask given the photographs," Faith asked, "but what was the cause of death?"

“Not silly to ask at all,” Garvey reassured her. “Check the last photo.”

Faith flipped to the last photo and gasped. The photo was a closeup of Harvey Harris’s neck. A blackened and blistered mark ran all the way around as though he had been strangled by a noose of fire.

“Jesus,” Michael whispered. “What am I looking at?”

“Electrical burn,” Garvey replied, “a really bad one. *That* is the cause of death for both victims.”

“Both victims?”

"Yes. It looks like a very large shock collar was slipped over their heads, and they were shocked to death with it."

“I didn’t think they made shock collars that powerful,” Faith replied.

“They don’t.” Garvey confirmed. “This would have to have been modified by the killer to push through far more amps than legally allowed. It wouldn’t take all that much, to be honest. He’d just have to pull out the electrodes from the collar and shove in something more powerful, like a cattle prod magnet or something. Either way, the coroner thinks we’re looking at anywhere from a quarter-amp to a full-amp of current at at least a thousand volts but probably more.”

Michael whistled. “This wasn’t a murder,” he said, “this was a message.”

“That’s what we believe,” Garvey said seriously. “We’re looking into other criminal gangs.”

“Top suspects?” Faith replied.

Garvey chuckled. “For something like this? I wish I could say this narrows the list down, but even the least powerful street gangs get creative when they’re sending a message. It could be anything from the Hansen Hellraisers to the Sinaloa Cartel.”

“Besides the body and the blood spatter,” Faith asked, “what evidence have you uncovered?”

“That’s it so far. The killer entered through the bedroom window, caught Harris smoking a bong in the living room and attacked him. Harris fought back hard, hence the destruction of his living room. At one point, he tried to escape. We found fingerprints on the front door and scuff marks from size fourteen work boots on the ground where the killer grabbed him and dragged him away.”

“Size fourteen?” Faith said.

“Lovely,” Michael added, “another freak of nature.”

Garvey grinned. “You didn’t think this job would be easy, did you?”

"Have you interviewed the neighbors?" Faith asked.

"There's no point," Garvey replied. "The answer is yes, we did, but all we got were variations on the theme of didn't see anything. Frankly, agents, Harvey could have been executed in the middle of the street while the killer broadcasted his name and street address via megaphone, and no one would have admitted to seeing anything. People who talk to cops get killed out here."

Faith looked again at the photos. She knew that Harvey Harris was far from a good man, but the image of his destroyed living room and the knowledge that he had fought for his life the way he did, only to succumb to a crazed killer, elicited a bout of sympathy for the man.

Gordon had died the same way.

Faith put the photos in her pocket and said, "What about the second crime scene?"

"That one's a little easier," Garvey replied. "That's Grant Street out past Maplewood. It's a poor neighborhood there, and I wouldn't expect anyone there to offer any more help than the people there, but it's not full of gangsters, and people keep their dogs on a leash. There's not much as far as evidence either, other than the cut fence and some bootprints, but I'll save you time on the boots. Size fourteen Doc Marten knockoffs, sold for thirty bucks in every warehouse store in the United States."

"They don't sell size fourteens in stores," Faith corrected.

Garvey shrugged. "They do here. You'll get the full report, of course, if you want to check my work. Between you and me, I think the gang connection is our best bet."

"Was Vinny connected to the Georgia Syndicate?" Faith asked.

"We haven't established a connection yet, but considering his past, I'm guessing it's more likely than not that he was working for them as a procurer."

"You mean a thief," Michael said.

"Yep. Funny how they don't like that word in the criminal world."

"I'd like to see the scene," Faith said, "and to interview the homeowner."

"That, at least, I can arrange."

***

Aloysius Farmer greeted the agents with a wan smile. As Garvey had said, the people of this neighborhood were less hostile than on

Hansen street, but that didn't mean they were friendly. Farmer's smile was the closest thing they had gotten to a polite greeting since arriving in Atlanta.

"Excuse the mess," he said as he led the agents to his backyard. "I haven't really had a chance to clean up since yesterday."

"That's understandable, Mr. Farmer," Michael replied. "I'm so sorry for what you've had to go through."

Farmer shrugged. "It's better than what the thief had to go through."

"Good point," Michael said.

"When did you discover Mr. Mariano's body?" Faith asked.

"Last night, when I got home from work. I get home late, around nine o'clock most days, but I was a little early yesterday on account of I had a cough."

"Got it," Faith said. "So what time were you home?"

"Seven-thirty."

"And you saw the body right away?"

"Yeah. I feed Macy when I get home. I was early, but I wanted to get to bed quick so the cough would disappear, so I headed out to feed her as soon as I got home. I found her passed out in her doghouse and the guy, the thief, dead."

"You said your dog was passed out?" Faith said.

"Yeah. The vet said there was a sedative in her body. It looks like someone knocked her out. I don't know if it was the thief or the murderer."

That would be an important question to answer.

"What did you do when you saw the body?"

"Well, I didn't know it was a body at first. I didn't see the hole in the fence or anything. I thought it was a homeless dude passed out in my yard. That happens sometimes."

"A lot of homeless people pass out in your yard?" Michael asked.

"Well, this is the first time it's happened to me, but I know two or three of my neighbors have come home to find people passed out on their couches or beds. I just figured it was the same thing."

"So what did you do?" Faith repeated.

Farmer sighed. "I walked over and said, 'Hey! What the hell you doin' boy? Get up out of my yard.' He didn't answer, obviously, so I…" he hesitated and glanced nervously at Garvey.

"Better you answer here than at the station," Garvey said.

Farmer nodded. "Well, I, uh, I kicked him."

"You kicked him?"

"Not hard," Farmer said, "just a little tap to wake him up. I didn't want to bend down and shake him in case he pulled a knife or something."

Faith and Michael exchanged a look. "So you kicked him, and then what?"

"Well, I saw his eyes all bloody and his neck all burnt up, and I realized he was dead."

"And that's when you called the cops?"

"Hell no," Farmer replied, "I got Macy, and I got out of the house as fast as I could. I drove to a coffee shop and called the cops from there. You gotta understand, agent, this isn't a good neighborhood. It's better than Hansen Street, but it's still not that safe. I was afraid that whoever killed that man might still be around."

That was understandable. "How long after discovering the body did you call the police?"

"I don't know," Farmer replied, "maybe fifteen minutes or so? I didn't really check."

Faith turned to Garvey, "and you responded to the call?"

"I did. It sounded an awful lot like the other case, and when I found out it was, I told my lieutenant I wanted on the scene."

"So what did you see?"

"Everything Mr. Farmer just described," she said. "The blood from the eyes was new. The killer used a lot more current this time."

"How's your dog?" Faith asked.

"She's good now. I'm keeping her inside for now. Probably for good. I don't know why they doped her up, but I don't want to risk her getting hurt. She's all I have."

Faith looked down at Turk, who had finished his inspection of the scene and now waited patiently for them to finish. "I know what you mean." She looked back at Mr. Farmer. "Do you mind if we see Macy for a moment?"

Farmer's brow furrowed. "Why?"

"Our K9 is trained to detect and remember specific scents. Even though the sedative is out of your dog's system, it's possible that traces might still remain on her fur or her breath. If Turk can recognize the scent, there's a possibility we can use it to track down the murderer."

Farmer looked ruefully at Turk. "Is he friendly?"

"As long as you and Macy are friendly, he's perfectly friendly," Faith replied.

He still looked unsure, but he nodded and said, “All right. She’s in the bedroom. I’ll bring her downstairs.”

He returned a moment later with an old Cocker Spaniel. The dog had red-brown fur with white paws and a white face with a liberal touch of gray on the muzzle. Faith guessed she was at least ten years old, probably older. Why would either of the men have bothered to sedate an old spaniel?

“Does Macy bark a lot?” Michael asked, evidently thinking the same thing.

“Almost never,” Farmer replied. “She’s the sweetest dog you’ve ever seen. I don’t know why they would have bothered doping her.” He chuckled affectionately. “Unless they were afraid of getting cuddled to death.”

Macy was indeed an affectionate dog. As soon as Farmer set her down, she trotted to the waiting agents and waited for pats, which the three of them were more than willing to give. Turk greeted her professionally, dipping his head and carefully sniffing around her. Macy accepted the inspection with good grace, and when Turk was finished, she licked his nose and trotted forward to lean her head against his.

Faith could almost swear that Turk blushed.

“She’s a sweetheart, isn’t she?” Farmer said, beaming at Macy with the love that humans reserved only for dogs and small children.

“She is,” Faith agreed with a smile. “Dogs are wonderful.”

“That they are,” he agreed emphatically. “I just don’t get why anyone would want to hurt them.”

“I’m glad Macy’s all right,” Michael said.

“Me too.”

They left Farmer then, sending Macy off with a round of farewell pats. On their way to the car, Garvey said, “I didn’t want to mention this while Mr. Farmer was present, but the killer continued to shock Mr. Mariano even after he was dead. The coroner said he was cooked on the inside.”

Michael shook his head. He looked sick. Faith looked back at the house and said, “This wasn’t just a gang hit. This was personal.”

CHAPTER SIX

At the hotel, Faith and Michael compared notes. Garvey gave them the coroner's report and the police report when she dropped them off, promising to keep them posted if she found anything else.

The report offered little information other than what they already knew. It provided some details such as the fact that the fence was cut with a pair of standard wire cutters and that the shock collar delivered its current via blunt metallic spikes, but the only somewhat useful piece of information was the coroner's belief that the killer was a fairly large and strong man, six-foot-three or -four and over two-hundred-twenty pounds. That made sense since Harris was fairly tall and muscular himself, and the killer had overpowered him.

Of greater interest was the gang connection. They would need to look into that first thing in the morning. Faith wasn't sure anymore that this was a simple hit. The injuries to the two men, especially to Mariano, were unnecessarily harsh, and the revelation that the killer had continued to shock Mariano's dead corpse was sobering. Whoever was doing this hated his victims. This stood in contrast to most of the cases Faith had worked, not because it was more brutal, but because the nature of the brutality didn't suggest insanity but simple hatred. The one case that came closest was the case in Arizona, ironically a case that also involved dogs.

"You think we have another white knight defending dogs?" Faith asked.

Michael shook his head. "I'm not sure. We don't really have a lot of hard evidence on the dog angle. The killer used a shock collar, and Farmer's dog was sedated, but we don't know if the killer sedated the dog or if Mariano did. And Harris didn't even have a dog. I think it might just be tangential."

Faith nodded. "You're probably right, but why sedate a dog that wasn't barking and wasn't even remotely capable of harming him? It doesn't make sense."

"The killer wouldn't know that Macy wouldn't bark."

"True, but how would he have managed to sedate the dog without Mariano noticing? He would have had to know that Mariano was going to be there ahead of time, sedate Macy, then wait for Mariano to arrive to kill him."

Michael sighed. "That would make Farmer the primary suspect except for his alibi. And it still doesn't explain why Mariano cut his way through the back fence or how the killer would have known he was going to be there."

"Maybe we're overthinking this," Faith suggested. "It could be that Mariano was going to steal Macy. So he sedates her, tries to steal her, the killer shows up and protects her."

"By putting a shock collar on him and frying him for dinner?" Michael countered. "No, you were right the first time. This is personal."

"So it's someone who's been hurt by the gang," Faith deduced.

"That's my guess. Someone wanted revenge, and this is how they got it."

"Well, that narrows our suspect pool down to anyone who's used cocaine in the American South in the past ten years along with all of their friends and families."

"Both victims were found in lower income neighborhoods in Atlanta," Michael said, "I think it's a safe bet our killer's from the same area. Probably a member of the gang or a former member or a family member of one. These aren't indiscriminate killings. He selected these two men. We don't know why, but he wanted these two gang members specifically. Harris was leadership, or at least middle management, but Vinny was just a contractor, not a part of the chain of command at all, and he was hurt worse than Harris."

"So how do we find out who wanted them dead?" Faith asked.

"Well, we can start by asking."

"You actually think they'll talk?"

"Probably not," Michael replied, "but we might be able to pick something up anyway."

***

As Michael predicted, the gang members wouldn't talk to them. Most of the known affiliates that Garvey rounded up for the agents in the morning simply said the word "lawyer" and clammed up. Even Turk's menacing growls didn't move them.

A few offered the opinion that it was none of the FBI's business. "H-Bomb was blood," a heavily tattooed man with a stout face told the agents. “When our blood is spilled, we’re the ones who spill blood back.”

“Are you threatening to retaliate?”

The tattooed man grinned. “I’m not threatening anything, agent. I’m just saying, you don’t need to worry about this. We’ll handle it.”

“Actually, we *do* need to handle this,” Michael said. “Two men are dead, brutally dead, and if you know anything, it will go a lot better for you and your friends if you just tell us.”

“You want to know what I know?” the man replied. “I know that as soon as you find the asshole who did this to H-Bomb, you’re going to ship him off to prison, then you’re going to pack up your shit and go home. And life here is going to go on. People die all the time on the streets, agents. You're not going to save anyone by poking your nose in where it doesn't belong."

“All the same,” Faith said, “we’re here, and like you said, we’re going to find the killer, and we’re going to send him to prison. The best thing you can do is cooperate with us.”

The man scoffed. "Cooperate? That's why you brought me to jail and sat me in an interrogation room with your dog growling at me every time I scratch my ass? You’re not here to cooperate with anyone, agent. Don’t try to play me like that.”

Faith and Michael shared an exasperated look. “All right, mister…”

“Snake Fist.”

“Mr. Snake Fist,” Faith said drily. “We’ll be in touch.”

They stood to leave. On their way out, Snake Fist called, “You have a lovely day, agents,” then cackled laughter at the closing door.

Faith, Michael and Turk returned to Garvey, who was watching from the other side of the mirror. Snake Fist grinned and offered both middle fingers to them even though he couldn’t see through the two-way glass.

“I take it he’s been here before,” Michael said.

“Yeah, Snake’s one of their pimps. We’ve had him in a half dozen times for pimping, dealing and assault, but the Syndicate has good lawyers. He’s never inside for more than a day or two.”

“If they have such good lawyers, why aren’t the lawyers here now?” Faith asked.

“They don’t usually show up until we charge somebody. It makes people look guilty if they go everywhere holding their counsel’s hand.”

Faith sighed. “Can we force any of them to talk? Threaten them with priors or something?”

Garvey shook her head. "Not unless we can think of a justifiable reason to detain them."

"Do you have anyone on the inside?" Michael asked. "A confidential informant or something like that?"

"Yeah, we have a CI," Garvey replied. "He's not 'in' the gang per se, but he hangs around them. Hears things, learns things, tells us enough to keep us from prosecuting him."

"Prosecuting him for what?"

"Well," Garvey said with a wry smile. "He's usually found at Black Betty's. That's a strip club downtown that's well known for providing other, less legal, services to well-paying customers. He'll run errands for the gang, and they'll pay him by giving him some of those services. We don't arrest him for solicitation as long as he gives us information when we need it."

"What's this CI's name?" Faith asked.

"Keenan Washington," Garvey replied. "Odds are, he'll be at the club already."

"At eleven in the morning?"

"Sure. He'll show up looking for work, take care of said work and return in the afternoon so he can… enjoy himself… before the girls have to get to work themselves."

"Sounds like a nice guy," Michael quipped.

"If you're looking for nice guys," Garvey replied, "you're looking in the wrong neighborhoods."

"Fair enough," Michael replied. "You have a car we can borrow, or do you want to come with?"

Garvey shook her head. "I want to lean on these guys a little more. Snake knows you're here temporarily, but he knows I'm here for life. He might be more willing to talk if I start suggesting that we double our patrols on his corner."

Faith frowned. "You're making deals with criminals?"

"Like Snake said," Garvey replied without animosity, "you get to leave when this is all over. I have to stay. Much as I would love to take a strong moral stance and bring the hammer of God down on everyone who sells dope and girls, I don't have the budget or the manpower. So we do the best we can."

Faith didn't reply, but her frown deepened.

"The car?" Michael reminded her.

“You can take one of the cruisers,” Garvey replied. “I don’t care which. The keys are hanging on the wall next to the bulletin board in the bull room.”

The key Michael picked turned out to be to a new Ford model police interceptor SUV. Faith didn't care much for the space-age cars that cops drove nowadays. Give her a good old-fashioned American V8 boat. Simple and modest, but it would run three hundred thousand hard miles as smooth as a kitten.

Michael, however, was relieved to drive something modern and comfortable after hours in an old beat-up Ford Bronco on leaf springs during their last case. He hummed a tune as he pulled into a drive-thru coffee shop.

“You really need coffee now?” Faith asked. “When we’re on our way to interrogate a person of interest?”

“Technically speaking, he’s a CI, not a person of interest,” Michael said, “and yes, I need coffee now.”

“Why didn’t you drink some at the station?”

“I said I need *coffee*, not brown water.”

Faith rolled her eyes. “Does Ellie put up with your snobbishness?”

“Ellie shares my snobbishness. She doesn’t even drink chain coffee anymore after I took her to Morning Glory.”

“Good for both of you,” Faith replied, “but if Keenan is out running drugs when we arrive, I’m going to hold you personally responsible.”

“Works for me,” Michael said cheerfully.

Twenty minutes later, coffee in hand—in both their hands, as Michael made sure to point out—they arrived at Black Betty. From the outside, the club looked like the worst dive bar Faith had ever seen. She hoped not to have to see the inside.

Fortunately, her prayers were answered when a man fitting Garvey’s description of Keenan Washington walked out of the club with a grin on his face. The grin vanished when he saw the three agents approaching. He looked around for a place to run to, but when he looked back at Turk, his better judgment took over. He lifted his hands and said, “I ain’t talking to cops.”

“We’re not cops,” Faith said, “I’m Special Agent Faith Bold and this is my partner, Special Agent Michael Prince. We need to talk to you.”

“That ain’t my problem,” Keenan said.

"Actually," Michael replied, "it is. Now, you can get in the car and come with us, or we can have this conversation in front of your boys. And your girls."

"You can have a conversation with my lawyer," Keenan said, jutting his jaw out."

Faith stepped closer so she could lower her voice. "Or we can have a conversation with your buddies inside," she said, "and tell them all about how much you actually *do* talk to cops."

Keenan flashed her an irritated glance and whispered, "Man, are you stupid? Arrest me. I can't be seen going willingly. You have to cuff me and take me somewhere else."

Faith and Michael shared an exasperated glance. Then Faith said, louder this time, "All right, Washington. Do you want to do this the hard way? I can make that happen. Turn around and put your hands behind your back."

"Man, fuck you guys," Keenan groused. "I'm tired of this shit. You guys always come harassing us and—"

"Quiet," Michael said and meant it.

Keenan clammed up but refused to turn and put his hands behind his back willingly, forcing Faith to turn him around and clamp the handcuffs on roughly. He protested again, muttering under his breath as they forced him into the car.

A small crowd had gathered in front of the club during this interaction. Faith looked at the flat-faced girls and the hard-eyed men and wondered what kind of life they must have lived to have so much animosity toward law enforcement.

As soon as they pulled out of sight of the club, Keenan said, "Okay, you can take the cuffs off now."

"We'll take them off when we stop," Faith said.

"Hey, come on. That wasn't the deal."

"We don't make deals," Michael said. "We ask questions, and you answer them, and if you don't, we make trouble for you. I strongly suggest that you don't make trouble for us."

Keenan scoffed. "Man, I work with Atlanta PD. What are you gonna do to me?"

"If you really feel you're untouchable," Faith replied, "Please test us."

Turk growled, and Keenan glanced nervously over at the passenger seat. "All right, all right. Look, I'm going to talk to you. Just can you please take the handcuffs off? It's cutting into my wrist."

"We'll be stopping in a few minutes," Michael said. "Hang tight."

"Man," Keenan whined. "You guys are assholes."

Faith had to bite her lip to keep from laughing.

Michael pulled into a diner a few minutes later, as promised, and Faith helped Keenan out of the car and took off the handcuffs. Keenan rubbed his wrists and pouted. "This better be good," he said, "I was going to hook up with Yadira today. You oughta see her. She's got tits the size of a—"

"I'll take your word for it," Faith said.

They ordered food and picked a booth near the back of the diner, away from listening ears. When they sat, Faith said, "All right, Keenan. Here's the deal. You're honest with me, I'm fair to you. You tell me what I need to know, and we get you out of here in time for a wonderful afternoon with Yadira, sound good?"

Here I am making a deal with a criminal, she thought.

"Yeah, all right," Keenan replied. "What do you want to know?"

"We want to know who killed Harvey Harris and Vincent Mariano."

"Well, I can't help you with Vinny," Keenan said. "I don't know what he did for the gang, but I know he didn't cross anyone. I also know he wasn't very high up. He was kind of like me, just a contractor. From what I've heard, he was good at whatever it was he did, and he never stole from anyone. I would say wrong place wrong time, but he got messed up real bad. So did H-Bomb."

"Tell me about H-Bomb," Faith said.

Keenan looked anxiously around the diner. Besides the three of them, there was an elderly couple enjoying a lunch date and a younger couple looking harried as they tried to corral three small children who were playing tag around the dining table. There was no sign of anyone suspicious.

He still lowered his voice when he said, "The Syndicate is pretty sure the Bulgarians are responsible for him."

"The Bulgarians?"

"Yeah, man. They're bad dudes. I heard that they had a beef with some guy down in Miami, and they hung him by his toes and took turns hitting him with a baseball bat. Like a pinata. Supposedly, only his legs were left by the time they finished with him. Everything else was spread all over the room."

Faith decided she wasn't hungry anymore. She set down her half-eaten sandwich and said, "Did Harris have beef with the Bulgarians?"

"That's what I heard. H-Bomb… he was… volatile, shall we say? He was better at making enemies than friends."

"What was the nature of their beef?" Michael asked.

"Girls, I'm guessing," Keenan replied. "H managed the street girls in Atlanta. The Bulgarians tried to muscle in a couple of times and H ran them out. The last time he got violent. They ended up beating one of the Bulgarians to death. Then he got cocky and warned the other gangs that they'd end up the same if they messed with him.

"And where was the Syndicate in all of this?" Faith asked. "Did they approve of H running his mouth like that?"

"They let their street captains figure their own stuff out," Keenan said. "As long as they don't bring trouble down on leadership or get the law involved, they stay out of the way. That's why there's no infighting. It's actually a pretty smart way to run things. They get their cut, and they get plausible deniability in case anyone does screw up."

"So why are people acting like they're going to avenge him?" Michael said. "If they like to keep distance between the street captains and leadership, why are people up in arms about Harris's death?"

"Those are all H-Bomb's crew," Keenan said, "Everyone in the projects is H's crew. The Syndicate—the leaders, anyway, they don't come anywhere near the streets. I don't think they're even in Atlanta. They probably live across the country in some mansions in Los Angeles, hobnobbing with celebrities and walking their designer poodles across the Hollywood Hills. See, you gotta stop thinking of the Syndicate as a gang. They're more like a mafia or a cartel. The street gangs pay them tribute and the Syndicate gives them access to lawyers and resources when they need it, but the people who call the shots—the real shots—you'll never see them."

CHAPTER SEVEN

They finished their lunch and left Keenan at the restaurant at his request. "You can't take me back to the club," he said, "then it looks like you chauffeured me. I gotta go back bitching about how you dumped me on the street when you couldn't get me to confess to anything and made me walk back. It looks bad enough that the FBI picked me up anyway."

"Might want to think about taking a night off from the club," Faith suggested, "just in case."

"Yeah," Keenan said ruefully. "Damn. I'm telling you, man, the best tits you've ever seen."

"A shame," Michael said drily.

Before they left, they got the name and last known address of one of the Bulgarians, a lieutenant named Iliev, who when things were going well, would supply the Syndicate with girls. Keenan suggested he might be willing to give the name of the trigger man in exchange for immunity.

Faith groused about that on the drive to the address listed. "It's like they're equals," she said, "like we have to talk to them like we owe *them* something and not the other way around."

"That's the way things are sometimes," Michael said. "I don't like it any more than you do, but New York, Chicago and L.A. all tried the strong-arm technique. It only made things worse for the little people caught in the crossfire, not to mention it increased gang participation tenfold in affected neighborhoods."

"So what do we do? Legalize drugs and prostitution and just let everyone do what they want?"

"There are some studies that suggest that exact solution," Michael said, "Take it out of the hands of the criminal underground and put it somewhere it can be regulated."

Faith stared at him. "What do *you* think?"

"I think I can't wait to get out of here," Michael replied. "The last time I was in Atlanta, I stayed in a nice hotel and visited nice places with nice people and great food—outstanding food. Saw a Falcons game and enjoyed some Georgia Peach Pie. I miss that Atlanta."

"Well, Philly has its rough places too, I suppose," Faith allowed.

"All cities do," Michael agreed, "but I don't have to visit them."

"Except when gang leaders are murdered," Faith said.

"That's the job."

They fell silent then. Turk slept in the back seat, and Michael envied the dog's ability to sleep anywhere at any time. He wished he had that kind of freedom.

Well, there was a way. He was a little less than five years away from twenty years, and then he would be fully vested in his pension. He hadn't considered retirement before, not seriously, anyway, but now that he was married, he wondered if advancement was really something he was cut out for. The Boss certainly didn't seem happy. Then again, it was hard to tell with the Boss. For all Michael knew, he wasn't capable of anything other than a scowl.

But did Michael really want to end up like that?

He looked over at Faith, who also rested. His face softened as he regarded the woman he loved as his best friend and at one time as more than a friend. The past two years had been very hard on them. Several times, Michael wondered if their friendship would survive. Even now, he wasn't sure about that. Faith had admitted finally that she was deeply affected by Trammell and West, but she had also admitted that she wouldn't stop hunting West, regardless of the consequences.

And what happened after that? At times, it seemed to Michael that West's existence was the only thing that kept Faith going. What would she do when the only remaining pillar of her existence was torn down, and by her own hands? Would she once more become the woman he knew, as she said she would, or would she be nothing more than a bitter, cynical shell? Michael had seen it happen to others before. Many of them didn't live long enough to grow old.

The problem was that West really was a threat. Michael had dismissed the urgency of his threats before, thinking him nothing more than a garden variety crackpot who was leaving letters behind like many killers did because of a warped and inflated ego that couldn't recognize how utterly foolish he seemed.

Now he knew better. West was still out there killing, and he was almost certainly doing so to torment Faith, exactly as she claimed he was. He had threatened David, he had threatened Michael, and he had threatened Ellie.

Michael's hands tightened around the steering wheel. Ellie had flatly refused to discuss an extended vacation with him. "I am *done* letting Frank control my life," she had said. "If he really wants to kill me, he can come try it. I have the shotgun, and I'll be more than happy to show him I know how to use it."

The shotgun was Ellie's one concession for her personal safety. It was a short-barreled twenty-gauge Remington, not the most powerful weapon but plenty for close-quarters self-defense and easier to handle than a twelve-gauge model, especially for someone as petite as Ellie.

Not that it would save her if West got the drop on her, as he almost certainly would. It worried Michael to be so far away from her. West, for all his bluster, was a coward. He lured Faith out to him rather than come to her. He wouldn't risk facing Michael. That, he believed, was an empty threat. Michael would admit that he wasn't the detective Faith was, but he was more than a match for most men in a fight, armed or unarmed, and most of his fantasies these days were about catching West alone and forcing him to pick a fight with someone his own size.

He smiled grimly as he imagined driving his fist over and over into West's face, hearing the satisfying crunch of cracking bones as he taught West why threatening and hurting the two most important people in his life was a very, very bad idea.

In moments like this, he could understand why someone would hate enough to kill another the way Mariano and Harris had been killed.

They reached the address a few minutes later. It was a working-class neighborhood, but not nearly as rundown as Hansen or Grant Street. Faith woke just as Michael parked the car, and Turk woke immediately after.

"That the house?" she asked.

"That's it," Michael said. "Let's try to be nice and calm at first. If we can get through this without a fight, that will be better than not."

Faith frowned at him. "I know that," she said, a little testily. "You don't have to tell me."

"I wasn't accusing you," he protested. "Sometimes I talk to calm myself down. You know this."

She rolled her eyes. "Well, grow a pair, will you? That's the job."

Michael glared at her for using his own words against him. "I should have dumped you and partnered with Rosa after all."

"Maybe I'll partner with Rosa," she retorted. "He looks like he could use someone experienced to show him the ropes. If you know what I mean."

Jeffrey Rosa was the newest agent at the field office. He was an attractive young man, and on a few occasions, Faith had caught him looking at her.

"Maybe we should ask David what you mean," Michael jibed.

"And maybe we should tell Ellie about your little infatuation with Chavez," she retorted.

The second-newest agent, Gloria Chavez, was a very attractive young woman, and on a few occasions, Faith had noticed her regarding Michael with a somewhat other-than-professional eye.

They cut the banter as they approached the house. Michael felt the hairs on the back of his neck prickle and drew his handgun.

Faith frowned at him. "I thought you said be calm."

"Shh," he said, "listen."

She fell silent. Turk stood in between them, ears up, tail switching slowly back and forth.

He was the first to pinpoint the danger. He barked and sprinted toward the back of the house. Faith and Michael followed him, guns drawn, hearts pounding.

It was moments like these that made Michael think more and more fondly of retirement.

They heard a scream and rounded the corner to see Turk's teeth buried in the forearm of a young man of medium height and build with close-cropped blonde hair and a tattoo of what Michael guessed was the Bulgarian flag on one shoulder. The hand attached to the forearm Turk was wrestling held a handgun.

Faith and Michael leveled their own weapons at the man. "Stand down, Iliev!" Faith shouted.

Iliev looked at her in shock and shouted something in Bulgarian.

"Drop your weapon," Faith warned, "Or I'll tell Turk to bite it off of you.

Iliev glared and tried to point his gun at them, but Turk yanked him to the ground. Iliev lifted his fist to strike Turk, but Michael reached him first, kicking Iliev's gun out of the way and pointing his own weapon at Iliev's nose.

Iliev glared at him, although that might have been a grimace since Turk's teeth were still buried in his arm.

"I think you know what I'm about to ask you," Michael said, "and I think you know the right answer to that question."

Iliev sighed and relaxed. "All right. You got me."

The agents kept their weapons trained on him as Turk released him and backed off. Blood seeped from Iliev's arm. He looked coolly at the wound and asked. "You mind if we go inside so I can clean this up? I'd rather not have to send you fine agents a hospital bill."

"No can do," Michael replied. "We have a first aid kit in the car, and I'm told that Atlanta PD has a fine nursing facility at every one of their precincts."

"And why, may I ask, am I being arrested?" he asked, sneering.

"For assault on an officer with a deadly weapon," Michael replied.

"Your dog attacked me first!"

"I doubt that," Faith said, "but feel free to lodge a formal complaint as long as you're all right with the FBI looking over every square inch of every place you've been for the past ten years to see if we can find a connection with you and the Bulgarian Mafia. I'm sure your employers would appreciate that."

"If you're here to talk about them," Iliev replied, "I'm afraid I can't help you."

"As a matter of fact," Michael replied, "we're here to talk about you."

Iliev looked between the agents, who continued to cover him with their weapons. Turk growled low in his throat, and Iliev decided he didn't want to risk another fight. "All right," he said, "Be careful with my right hand, please." He curled his lip in contempt. "It's bleeding."

CHAPTER EIGHT

Bogdan Iliev looked at the two agents with the easy contempt that all professional criminals showed law enforcement. Only Turk seemed to command his respect, which didn't surprise Faith, considering how effortlessly Turk managed to take him down. He glanced at the dog nervously before remembering himself and turning a haughty glance back up to the agents.

"Okay, Iliev," Faith said, "Tell us why you're here."

"That's your job, madam agent," Iliev said with a contemptuous smile.

Faith shrugged. "Suit yourself. You're here because you're a person of interest in the murders of Harvey Harris and Vincent Mariano."

Iliev blinked in surprise.

"Not expecting that, were you?" Michael asked.

Iliev, showing surprising candor, replied, "No. Honestly, I thought you were here about the drugs. That's why people always talk to me. They assume that just because I have tattoos and carry a pistol, I must be a drug runner."

"Are you a drug runner?" Michael pressed.

He grinned, "So it *is* about the drugs."

"No, it isn't," Faith said. "Personally, I don't care if you're running drugs. That's not what I'm here for. I'm here for the two people who were shocked to death in the past week."

He chuckled. "A nice piece of artistry, that. A shock collar? That's just beautiful."

Faith leaned forward. "I get that you have to pretend to be arrogant and unmoved by our threats, but I think it will serve you better to just answer our questions without acting like an idiot. Shall we try that?"

"I don't know what to tell you," Iliev replied. "It wasn't me. It wasn't anyone I knew, either by sight or by name. Honestly, I wish it was. That's a beautiful way to send a message. Whoever did it just earned a lot of street credit."

"You haven't heard anything about it?" Michael asked. "Anyone enjoy a sudden spike in 'street credit'?"

Iliev chuckled. "Not that I know of. If you were asking my opinion, I would say it's someone within the Syndicate. You are aware that Harris was a man of some stature within the Syndicate, aren't you?"

"We know he ran the street crew here," Faith said.

"Not just the street crew," Iliev replied. "The clubs, the hookers and the dog fights too."

Faith's ears perked up. "Dogfights?"

"Oh yes. You haven't heard about the dogfights? That was Harris's big moneymaker. Well, the girls were his big moneymaker. They always are. The one thing that poor people want—any people really—more than drugs is sex. You control sex, you control a territory. That's why the Syndicate is so powerful in Atlanta. You earn a lot of highly placed friends if you can provide willing girls. If you know what I mean."

Faith knew what he meant, but she wasn't here to bust a prostitution ring either. "Tell me about the dogfights."

"I can't. I wasn't allowed anywhere near them. Only Harris's crew could be involved with dogs, just like only Harris's crew could be involved with girls. My… associates… preferred that I keep the peace with Harris. They were very clear that there was to be no retaliation for the altercation where Harris killed one of our own. From what I understand, they accepted a seven-figure settlement from the Syndicate and left it at that."

Faith and Michael glanced at each other. This was becoming more complicated than they had expected. "What about Mariano?" Michael asked. "What did he have to do with the dogs?"

"No clue. I know he was involved, but how? I couldn't guess."

Faith could. She had an idea now why Farmer's fence was cut open and his dog sedated.

But why would a dog fighting ring want an old, sweet Cocker Spaniel? Macy was about as far from a fighting dog as Faith was from a sumo wrestler. Unless people just liked watching big dogs eat small dogs. She wouldn't put that past them.

"What else can you tell us about the Syndicate?" Faith asked. "Who's in charge now that Harris is out?"

Iliev chuckled. "Agents, I know I look like an attractive and capable leader, but the truth is, I'm fairly low on the ladder. If anyone I know has the information you seek, they haven't told me, and they won't. I get orders, and I follow them. I do a very good job of following them, and I do a very good job of not being nosy. That's why I'm still alive."

“Who could we talk to who might know the answers?” Faith asked.

Iliev met her eyes. “Not answering questions like that is another reason I’m still alive.”

Faith sighed and said, “All right, Mr. Iliev. We’re going to hold you until we decide if we’re pressing charges for the assault on our persons.”

Iliev chuckled and rolled his eyes. “Of course you are.”

“Count yourself lucky it isn’t worse than that,” Faith said. “Yet.”

As they left the room, Iliev called after them. “Good luck on your collar, agents.” He laughed at his on joke, and Faith was relieved when the door closed and blocked the sound of his voice.

***

“You lied to us, Keenan,” Faith said.

“I told you!” he replied, his face slick with the sweat of desperation. “I didn’t lie to you. I don’t know anything!”

Faith leaned over the table and stared hard at him. Michael showed the same stony glare, and Keenan paled a shade. His eyes shifted to the left, telling Faith that she was right to suspect him of lying. "All right, Keenan," she said, "Here's what's going to happen. We're going to take you to the precinct, where you'll be charged with obstruction of justice."

He paled another shade but somehow managed a defiant look. “You can’t threaten me. The cops use me as an informant. I’m valuable to them.”

Faith hadn’t worked with CI’s before, but she was willing to bet that Keenan wasn’t nearly as valuable as he thought he was. Still, she would much rather he talked now than force them to go through the hassle of charging him and performing a formal interrogation.

She looked at Michael, who nodded and said, “that’s a good point, Keenan. Here’s another idea. We drive you back to the club, where we thank you loudly and publicly for your help in the Harris case and promise you that as long as you continue to provide valuable information to us, we’ll see to it that you’re handsomely rewarded for your trouble.”

Keenan looked like he might be sick.

“I like that idea,” Faith said. “Clap you on the shoulder, call you a good citizen, tell you to enjoy your night with Yadira. Yeah, that sounds like a plan.”

"You two are evil," Keenan complained. "You know that?"

"You don't want to talk to us about evil," Faith said.

Keenan sighed and ran his hands through his hair. He shook his head bleakly and said, "You know you could be getting me killed by asking me this stuff, right?"

"I know that people are already getting killed," Faith countered, "and that you know more than you told us the last time we talked. That makes me a lot less concerned about your safety."

"All right," he said, "I get it. Fine." He looked around the diner, where once more, there was only the odd elderly couple and harried family of below-school-aged children. "Look, I'm not supposed to know this, okay? I don't just mean I'm not supposed to tell you, I mean I'm not supposed to know it in the first place."

"And we care about that because…?" Michael said.

"I know you don't care," Keenan spat. "But I do, and that means if I'm going to tell you, I need some guarantees."

"You're not in a position to demand anything, Keenan," Faith said.

"Well, if people find out it's me talking, I'm going to get killed, and then you'll have a new murder to solve. So how about we save me some pain and you some work, and you promise me that my name never comes up. You don't even use the word CI. You don't talk about sources. You just say that you learned this fact or discovered that fact and leave it at that. Can we agree on that, at least?"

"You give us something useful," Faith said, "and you have my word I forget your name and face the moment this case is over."

"Good," Keenan said. He turned to Michael. "What about you?"

"Believe me, kid, I have better things to do than railroad a two-bit john. You help us out, I will gladly erase the memory of you from my mind."

"The feeling is mutual, agent," Keenan replied.

He looked at Turk, who watched him with a calm, half-bored expression.

After a moment, Keenan nodded and said, "Okay. Here's what I know. Harris ran a dog-fighting ring in the inner city. He had his boys handle it: finding locations, finding dogs, setting up fights, taking bets, collecting, all that stuff. You know how the mob used to run boxing back in the day?" Faith nodded. "Well, it's the same thing here. You want to fight dogs in Atlanta, you go through H. Or at least, you used to. Now that he's out, I have no idea what'll happen. There's a power vacuum and a half going on now. If you think it's good riddance that H is out of the picture, you have another thing coming. Things are gonna get heavy here real quick."

"So Harris ran the ring," Faith interjected, "What about Vincent Mariano? What's his connection?"

"I honestly don't know," Keenan said, "I know he was an errand boy for them. I know he was a little more… respected… of an errand boy than me."

"Meaning?"

"Meaning I do intern shit. Bring me coffee, bring me lunch, bring me drycleaning… stuff like that. Mariano did actual work for them, but I don't know what."

"So you couldn't tell me if he ever procured dogs for Harris?"

"No," Keenan said, "I can't tell you what he did ever besides refuse a lapdance from Carla. Can't trust a man who don't want no lapdances from Carla. She's got an ass like—"

"Let's not talk about girls," Michael said, "case only."

"I mean, I don't really know anything else," Keenan said, "Just that Mariano worked for them running errands. If you want my opinion, I'll tell you that I'm pretty sure he was running dogs just like he was running drugs and girls, but I don't think you want my opinion."

"Almost never," Faith agreed, "but in this case, I think you might be right. I want you to ask around and see what you can learn about this ring. I'll be back to talk to you later."

Keenan chuckled mirthlessly. "You don't know nothing about gangs, do you, agent? You don't ask around for anything. You hear things, and unless the things you hear are said about you or to you, you act like you didn't hear them. I can keep my ears open, but I doubt like hell I'm going to hear anything about the dogs."

"I don't think that's true," Faith said. "There's a power vacuum now. People are going to be looking to fill that vacuum. That means they're going to be looking for people to support them. That means they're going to talk. You don't need to ask questions if you think it's going to get you killed, but you need to listen. I'm pretty sure you'll learn something. When we talk to you again, I'll be very interested in what you have to say."

"When will that be?" Keenan asked.

"When we show up," Faith replied.

CHAPTER NINE

“It’ll have to be Michael,” Garvey said, “No one will believe you’re a dogfighter.”

“Why not?” Faith asked.

“You’re too pretty,” Garvey said. “People will look at you and think you’re a cute little girl. They won’t take you seriously, and believe me, these men need to take you seriously for your own safety.”

"Thank you for the compliment, but I can handle myself," Faith said. "If they want to treat me like a cute little innocent girl, they'll be in for a big surprise."

“That’s what I’m afraid of,” Garvey replied. “If you show up with Turk acting like you want to fight him, someone’s going to make some joke about you being a nice piece of ass and suggest you show him how badly you want to be in the club. When that happens, you’ll probably beat the hell out of him, and when you do, that will end any chance of us getting info on the gang, the dog fights or the murders. It has to be Michael.”

Faith frowned, but she knew Garvey was right. “Okay,” she said, “so how do we get Michael inside?”

After talking with Keenan the second time, the two agents concluded that the only way to get the information they needed to find their killer was to send one of them undercover. Turk could play the part of a fighting dog easily. In a way, he was a fighting dog, just a much better-trained one. And he had the scar on his face and the chipped tooth, wounds sustained from the Donkey Killer and the Copycat Killer respectively. Faith thought he was the handsomest dog that ever lived, but when he was ready to fight, he was terrifying.

Apparently, Faith herself wasn’t. She didn’t think of herself as the pinnacle of beauty, but she had to admit that her trim figure and relatively soft features didn’t exactly scream hardass. Michael, on the other hand, didn’t look particularly dangerous, but Faith knew he was tough and brave and more than willing to meet the eyes of anyone who wanted to test him.

And he was a very dangerous fighter. That wasn’t a skill they had to call upon often, but unless their killer turned out to be a freak like the

Cave Dweller from their last case, Faith was confident that if it came to a scuffle, Michael would be the one left standing.

"If we want to get Michael inside," Garvey said, "then we need to make him look dangerous. That means a haircut, no more facial hair, and he has to dress like a gangster, not like Dick Tracy."

Michael cast her an injured look and took off his fedora. "Is the shave really necessary? Ellie likes this beard."

"Ellie's your wife?" Garvey asked.

"Yeah."

"Well, your wife likes your beard because it makes you look adorable and harmless," Garvey said, "two qualities we don't want in a badass dogfighter. So the beard goes."

He sighed. "She's going to kill me for this."

Garvey cracked a smile. "I don't know about that. Sweet girls always think they want sweet guys until they meet bad boys. If I were you, I'd try to bring the badass look home. I'll bet you anything Ellie will be naked faster than you can close the door behind you."

Faith chuckled at Michael's blush. "Well, I suppose I'll have to let that be enough to comfort me," he said, "What about Turk? Is he going to be believable as a fighting dog? He's trained not to fight unless commanded."

"Can he look like he wants to fight?" Garvey asked. "He already looks scary with that scar and the snaggletooth."

"We can work on something," Faith said.

"Good." Garvey smiled again. "I have to say, you two have turned out to be a lot cooler than I expected. The feds I've worked with in the past are usually stuffy and holier than thou. It's nice to work with feds who don't mind getting their hands dirty."

"Always happy to help," Michael said with only the slightest touch of sarcasm.

"Good. Here's what we're gonna do."

***

Faith and Turk headed back to the hotel while Garvey took Michael back to Black Betty to pick up Keenan. Keenan would arrange a meeting for Michael with the leaders of the dogfighting ring. Michael was now Michael Ponce. He was from Los Angeles and was now in Atlanta looking for a place to ply his trade.

Meanwhile, Faith would teach Turk how to look like a fighting dog. The problem was that she had no idea what a fighting dog would look like. She knew what a dog looked like when it was fighting, but knowing what such a dog looked like outside of the ring was not something she was familiar with.

Fortunately, a few internet searches gave her all the info she needed. The dogs in the videos basically acted like animals whose only reason for existing was to tear other animals limb from limb. There was a lot of snarling, bristling, snapping, growling and posturing, especially when they were around other dogs.

The hardest part would be to get him to look simultaneously as though he were afraid of Michael, obedient to him and also as though he hated Michael to his very core and would tear his throat out if only he wasn't certain that Michael would hurt him if he tried.

Turk barked enthusiastically and Faith turned to see him wagging his tail and bouncing up and down as a dog on tv ran through an obstacle course. He turned to her, his goofy open-mouthed smile and exuberant eyes the polar opposite of the dogs Faith saw online.

Faith admired his strength. He had been hurt badly by West, and worse by Trammell before him, but he was still a puppy at heart. Even though he was a Marine Corps dog turned FBI K9, Faith imagined he would be more at home playing hide and seek with some kids than fighting other dogs.

But here he was, after suffering at least as much trauma as Faith herself, and he was still joyful, still happy just to be around his human, no matter what they were doing.

Faith's smile faded as she thought of him fighting some massive dog in the ring. She trusted Turk to come out on top in any fight, but what if he didn't? West had shown her that Turk wasn't invincible. If he slipped or ended up with the wrong dog, he could get hurt or killed far too swiftly for Michael to intervene.

God, she hated this.

But it was their best chance at solving this case. If Turk could understand, Faith knew he would tell Faith to let him help, to let him do what Faith had done so many times and put himself at risk to help catch a killer.

She thought of David's words to her earlier. He told her that it worried him to know that she regularly put her life in danger for the sake of her job, but that she would never ask her to quit because he knew she wouldn't. She took her job seriously and had long since understood that it might mean she died someday.

Turk was no different. Just because he was a dog didn't mean he didn't know what danger was. He had already put his life in danger for Faith's sake dozens of times. Faith knew he wouldn't shy away from this job either.

She got up and switched off the tv. Turk protested with a whine and Faith said, "I'll put the show on later. Right now, I need to teach you something."

She made a little space in the hotel room, pushing the chairs and the bed apart. Turk cocked his head questioningly, and she said, "This will all make sense in a moment. Okay, Turk. Heel."

Turk cocked his head again, but other than that remained completely still.

"Sit."

Turk sat.

"Listen."

Understanding crossed Turk's face. That was the same sequence of commands they used when they were training him for Faith's K9 certification. He dutifully sat and paid attention.

Faith turned the laptop to him and said, "Be mean."

He cocked his head, and Faith played a video of a dog snarling and snapping at someone through a fence. The dog was chained and straining against the leash. Turk watched intently, and Faith repeated the command. "Be mean."

She played the video again. When it concluded, she paused the laptop and said, "Be mean."

Turk stared at her, concentrating hard. Finally, he took a tentative step forward and placed his paw on the laptop. He looked at her questioningly, and she sighed. "Let's try again."

She closed the laptop and pointed at herself. "Faith, be mean."

She growled at Turk, snapping and biting. Turk stared at her as though she had suddenly gone crazy and barked in concern.

"Yeah, I don't blame you," she said. She side and said, "Okay, one more try."

She opened the laptop and played the video again. "This dog is mean," she said.

Turk stared intently at the screen, and Faith said, "this dog is mean."

Turk barked to indicate understanding, and Faith said, “All right. Turk, be mean.”

Turk looked at her for a long moment. Then he barked tentatively. He bared his teeth uncertainly, and Faith said, "Yes! Be mean, Turk! Just like that."

Turk growled a little more convincingly. Faith glared at him to demonstrate the anger she wanted to see. “Be mean.”

Turk barked loudly and growled more angrily. “Good,” Faith said. “Be mean. Be really mean.

Turk lunged at her so suddenly and convincingly that she cried out and stumbled backward. Turk glared at her and barked and snarled, ears flat back on his head. He lunged at her again, stopping himself just before reaching her so his jaws snapped inches from her face. He continued this for a few moments, then sat back and barked in a much more friendly and calm manner.

Faith smiled at him. “Good boy. Be mean.”

He resumed the act, so convincingly that even though Faith knew that he was pretending, the hair on the back of her neck still rose. “You’re good at this,” she said.

Turk barked happily at the praise and looked up at her with the soft, beautiful brown eyes that had stolen her heart two years ago.

“Okay,” she said. “I think we’re ready. But just in case, let’s practice again. Be mean.”

Turk grinned in excitement, then barked and snapped threateningly once more.

Faith’s heart pounded with fear, but she pushed her fear aside and smiled. “Good dog.”

She tried to keep her smile, but all she could picture was Turk in the middle of a pile of vicious dogs as they tore him limb from limb.

She knelt down and pulled him close. “Good dog.”

CHAPTER TEN

Franklin West looked out the window of the cabin in the mountains and thought for the hundredth time how beautiful it was out here. People didn't give California enough credit for its natural beauty. Everyone was preoccupied with the cities and the beaches. He supposed the beaches were beautiful, but when people thought of California beaches, they didn't think of the waves or the soft sands, they thought of bleach blonde girls with manufactured bodies stuffed into undersized bathing suits and godlike men with wavy blonde hair and a tan that would eventually turn into malignant skin cancer, a dry cloak of calloused leather or both.

No one thought of the clear mountain air, the moon shimmering through the undulating pine forests. No one thought of the vast and imposing deserts, the acres of poppies in the southern valleys, or the rolling hills of the central inland paradise.

No, California, like so many places, had been commercialized and turned into a Hollywood caricature of progress, at least in the minds of everyone who lived outside of the state. It was too bad he had killed Sergeant Decker here. He would have loved to stay.

Oh well. Maybe when he retired. If he retired.

A part of him *was* retired, at least as far as the rest of the world was concerned. Franklin West had been his favorite personality, so much so that he thought of himself as West now.

The problem was that everyone now knew that Franklin West was the Copycat Killer, the serial murderer whose exploits had become so notorious that most didn't even remember who he was supposed to be copying. He could no longer work under that guise.

So, once more, he had to change himself. He stood on the balcony for a moment longer, then sighed and headed inside.

His tools were laid out on the bathroom sink. The prosthetics were easily obtained through a costume company. Halloween was in three weeks, and no one thought to ask why a man in his forties would want to change his appearance to look ten years older and thirty pounds heavier. He didn't even need to use the story about dressing as a famous serial killer for Halloween.

Which was for the best. It was a bit of arrogance to make up a story about being a different murderer for Halloween. It was unlikely that it would have raised eyebrows, but still, any risk was too much risk with Faith Bold hunting him.

He would miss the goatee, though. He thought it made him look distinguished.

He wouldn't miss the brown eyes. There was something about gray eyes he had always loved. They were just… well, he didn't know what to call it.

Vast. That was it. They were vast. Like the California desert. Like the Sierra Nevadas. Like the Pacific Ocean. They were vast, and when he placed the contacts carefully over his eyes, he looked into his reflection and saw a vast, all-consuming gaze.

He smiled at that and lifted his razor.

"Goodbye, Franklin West."

CHAPTER ELEVEN

Faith tapped her earpiece and said, "Michael, do you copy?"

"Loud and clear," Michael said softly, "you read me?"

"Gotcha," Faith said, "What do you see?"

"Not much yet," Michael said, "the crowd is what you'd expect. A bunch of street toughs walking around and posturing, trying to prove they're the toughest cock in the henhouse. I wonder if any of them look in the mirror?"

"I can't imagine the life of a criminal is one that inspires self-reflection," Faith said. "How's Turk?"

"He's okay. He seems nervous, but I can't tell if that's him being in character, or if he's really nervous."

"Does he seem nervous, fearful, or nervous like he's ready to rip something apart at any moment?"

"Definitely the second one."

"Then he's in character. What about you? Are you in character?"

"Well, I look like I sell weed to college kids and blast death metal from my old Ford Econoline van at stoplights. Does that count?"

Faith smiled. "That works."

She tapped her earpiece twice to mute it, then turned to Garvey in the seat next to her. "Do we have a lock on him?"

"GPS has him," Garvey said, "Since he's indoors, it won't be accurate within more than ten or fifteen feet, but we have him."

"What about microwave?" The microwave transmitter was more sensitive than the GPS, especially in close quarters.

"No luck there," Garvey said. "The receiver's fried."

Faith swore and double-tapped her earpiece again. "Michael, the microwave's fried. We're relying on GPS."

"That's fine with me," he said. "Are you expecting trouble?"

"I'm expecting tension," she said. "Hopefully it doesn't go any farther than that."

"Well, I'll do my best not to look anxious," he said. "I have to tell you, I stick out like a sore thumb, though."

"That's okay," Faith said. "You're from California. You don't need to look like them, you just need to look like you belong."

"Where are you guys parked?"

"We're two warehouses down and one across," Faith said, "about a half mile away. We're hidden from view, so no one wonders what a gray van is doing loitering across the street."

"Good," he said, "Gotta go. Someone's coming with a dog. I need to act like Turk's straining at the leash. What's the command again?"

"Be mean," Faith repeated.

"Got it. Turk, be mean. Jesus!"

Faith couldn't resist a smile as she heard Michael struggle with the leash while Turk barked and snarled. She heard an anxious voice on the other end say, "Hey, keep your dog in line, man. It ain't his turn tonight."

She double tapped her earpiece to mute it but kept listening to Michael. "How about you take your dog away before Turk decides to have an evening snack?"

"Motherfu—"

"Jamal!" a third voice interrupted. "What are you doing up here? Bruiser's the third fight. Get his ass—and yours—down to the damned pit! Sorry about that, Mike. This Turk?"

"Easy, Turk," Michael said, the command for Turk to stop being mean. "Yeah, this is him."

The new voice scoffed. "He looks like a bitch."

"Yeah?" Michael replied. "Bring Bruiser back here, and I'll show you how much of a bitch he is."

Faith knew it was just an act, but she tensed anyway. Michael was just a guest tonight, watching the fights to see if he believed it was a good place for him to make money with his dogs, but he was surrounded by legitimate gangsters with legitimate dogfighters, and while backup wasn't far, it might as well have been on the other side of Canada. They wouldn't get to Michael or Turk fast enough to help them if something went down.

"Your boy's laying it on a little thick," Garvey said.

"What should he do?" Faith asked.

The answer to their question came when the stranger chuckled. "Relax, Mike, relax. You want Bruiser, you're gonna have to earn him. Bruiser's a champion. You gotta work your way up."

"Didn't look like much of a champion to me. Jamal looked ready to shit a brick when he saw Turk."

Faith double tapped her earpiece and said, "Easy, Michael. Don't provoke anyone."

"Chill the ego, man," the other voice said. "I get that you got shit to prove, but right now, you just a spectator, *comprende?* Just sit back, have a beer, have a girl, and enjoy the show. Oh. Your dog's gotta stay in the cages, though. Can't have fighting dogs in the crowd during the fights. We tried that once, and it wasn't pretty. We got a spot reserved for him."

Faith bristled and nearly told Michael not to let that happen, but Garvey grabbed her shoulder and shook her head. Faith frowned, but she relented. She knew this was probably going to happen. She didn't relish the idea of Turk being alone, but they wouldn't put two fighting dogs in the same cage.

"Michael, tell Turk to be mean when you put him in the cage. Make it seem casual."

"Got it," Michael said. "See you later, Gaucho."

Faith muted her microphone and Garvey said, "Francisco Jimenez, nickname, Gaucho. He's the pit boss."

"Could he have murdered Harris?"

"Possibly, but I don't know why he would have murdered Mariano too. Mariano was so far down on the ladder he wasn't even on it. It would be like killing a man, then killing his pet fish."

Except Mariano wasn't a fish, he was a man. Faith understood her point, though. "How long do these fights usually run?"

"An hour or two," Garvey said, "they aren't worried about cops too much, but they know better than to make enough noise to attract attention. They'll do their business, collect their money and get out."

Faith nodded and turned to the monitor, where an orange dot indicated Michael's position and a green dot indicated Turk. The green dot remained stationary since Turk was in a cage now, and the orange dot moved steadily away.

***

Michael hated this. He wasn't good at undercover. He had studiously avoided any career track that would require him to go undercover. He grew up in an upper-middle-class neighborhood in the San Francisco Bay and had attended school in Berkeley before joining the FBI. He knew about as much about life on the street as he did about oil futures.

And he really didn't like that Turk was separated from him. Turk was a great dog, but Michael doubted that Turk would understand to stay mean for the entire time it took Michael to watch the fights.

Michael risked trying to move the meeting up. "Hey, Gaucho, I don't want to be a pain, but when do I meet the organizers?"

Gaucho laughed. "Patience, *ese.* Come on, man, I thought people were chill in California. Watch the fights, enjoy yourself. Hey, Trixie!"

A buxom young woman wearing far too little clothing for a cool night like tonight plastered a seductive smile underneath supremely bored eyes. "Yes, Daddy?"

"Bring my friend Mike a drink. Make it nice and sweet for him, okay?"

Trixie looked Michael up and down with practiced sultriness. "Ooh, he's cute."

"Tell him that after you bring him his drink, baby," Gaucho said with a grin.

I'm sorry, Ellie, Michael thought as he forced himself to watch Trixie walk away.

"She's cute, huh?" Gaucho said.

"She's something," Michael replied.

Gaucho laughed. "Wait until you see what she can do with those hips. I hope you ate a good breakfast, *muchacho.* You're gonna need your strength."

He laughed again and Michael managed a smile as Gaucho led them to their "seats," a couple of overturned crates a few yards back from the ring.

Michael's first dogfighting experience was even more traumatic than he expected. The show didn't start with a fight as he expected. Instead, a small Pomeranian was released into the ring and left to quail in fear for over a minute while the announcer introduced the fighters, a Rottweiler named Brutus and a Dobermann named Killer.

Michael would have nightmares for a long time after hearing the noises coming from the ring.

"They have bait dogs in California?" Gaucho asked, "Or do they just starve the dogs?"

"We just starve 'em," Michael said, "Makes them ready to fight anything."

"Yeah, but it kills their stamina," Gaucho said. "That's why we started using bait dogs. Gets their blood up, but it's not enough food to make them sleepy. They start fighting each other, and they have the energy to go forever. Not that they do. They end up dead—well, one of them does—within a minute or two."

Sure enough, Killer lived up to his name, and after less than two minutes, he walked away from the mangled body of Brutus. Trixie returned with his drink and, of course, sat on his lap and wiggled her hips. He managed to do a passable job of seeming interested, all the while reminding himself that this was necessary to catch a murderer.

Michael endured one more fight but didn't get to see the legendary Bruiser defend his title. Gaucho tapped his shoulder and said, "All right, Impatient Mike. The bosses want to see you now."

Michael scratched his ear, tapping his earpiece as he did. "Wonderful. Where are we meeting them?"

"They have a room upstairs," Gaucho said. "You'll have to leave Trixie behind, though."

Michael turned to her and forced a lecherous grin. "I'll see you soon, baby."

Trixie nibbled his earlobe and said, "Don't keep me waiting long."

God help Michael, but he would personally see everyone here thrown in prison.

Gaucho led him to the cages. "We're getting your dog," he said, "They're going to want to see what Turk can do."

Michael paled. He feared suddenly that Turk would be asked to eat a bait dog, something that couldn't and wouldn't happen. Faith must have feared the same thing because she said, "If you need us, tap. Try to give us five minutes to show up, but we should be there in two."

He was mildly encouraged to see Turk still snarling and snapping at the other dogs. A few of the other dogs even cowered against the corners of their cages.

"Pinche cabrones," Gaucho said, "Hey, Jose. Get these little bitches out of my cages."

Jose obliged, calling on his radio for handlers to help him with the dogs who cowered. Gaucho smiled at Turk and said, "He's a killer, huh? Damn. Usually shepherds are too small for this kind of fighting, but I think Turk here might surprise us. You know that German Shepherds are related to wolves?"

As are all dogs, Michael thought drily. Aloud, he said, "That so? Explains why he howls all damn night."

Gaucho threw his head back and howled himself. Then he laughed and clapped Michael on the shoulder. "Just you wait, Mike. Five minutes with Trixie, and she'll have you howling just like Turk."

He howled again, and Michael joined him to keep up appearances. *God, I hate you, you bastard.*

He followed Gaucho up to the office where three men and—surprisingly—a woman waited. They wore the stony expressions of hard businessmen who knew that their work could get them and many others killed or thrown in prison.

"All right, Mike," Gaucho said when Michael and Turk entered. "This here's my boy, Mike. He's from L.A. He's got this dog here, Turk. Says Turk's a champ. Says he's gonna make Bruiser look like a little bitch."

Turk growled menacingly, and Michael looked over the room, wondering which of the men Turk had picked out as a suspect. It worked for the charade, and the woman nodded at Gaucho, who clapped Michael on the shoulder and said, "Have fun, man. I'll keep the dogs away from Trixie, if you know what I mean.

He laughed and howled again on his way out the door. Michael turned back to the four. This would be the riskiest part.

"All right," he said, "You said you want to see what Turk can do. So who's he eating?"

CHAPTER TWELVE

Two of the men chuckled briefly, rather impressive considering their expressions didn't change. The man who didn't chuckle said, "He's too small. Even if he's mean, he's not going to make it in there with a hundred-twenty-pound Rottweiler."

"He's fought Rottweiler's before and won," Michael said, which was technically true even if the dogs in question weren't actually trying to kill him.

"So you say," the woman said, "but what you say doesn't mean shit. We don't know you."

Michael grinned cockily. "Hi. I'm Michael Ponce. I train champion fighting dogs. This dog is going to kill your champion Rottweiler and any other bitch you throw in with him."

"Really?" one of the men said sarcastically. "Right now, he's wagging his tail like he's waiting for a treat."

Turk was indeed wagging his tail, but not like he was waiting for a treat. He was staring directly at the only man who hadn't spoken yet, his eyes boring into him. Michael glanced over him and said, "Looks like he found one."

The man curled his lip contemptuously. "You threatening me, white boy?"

Michael whispered, "Be mean."

Turk didn't respond.

Michael turned his grin at the man and lifted his hands. "I'm not threatening anyone. Don't worry, Turk will do what I say. I won't let him hurt you."

The four of them laughed. The woman said, "We haven't seen him hurt anything. You say he can fight. Well, show us."

Michael shrugged. "All right."

He looked at Turk and said, "Turk. Be mean."

Turk still didn't respond. Michael felt beads of sweat forming on his forehead.

The men looked at each other. The woman scowled at Michael.

“What is this, a cartoon?” one of the men asked derisively. “Come on, man, show us something or get your bitch ass out of here before we shoot you.”

Come on, Turk, Michael said.

He met the man’s eyes and said, “Bad idea. Turk? Be mean.”

This time, thank God, Turk did what he was told. He lunged at the man, teeth bared, jaws snapping, so quickly that Michael himself was terrified. The four organizers all jerked backward, eyes wide with alarm.

“Stop!” Michael cried.

Turk stopped inches from the man’s face. He whined and growled, and when the man eased back slightly, he barked and snapped at him.

“Don’t kill him, Turk,” Michael said, his cocky grin returned. “He needs to pay us money.”

Turk growled and bunched his shoulders in a perfect imitation of being irritated at holding back.

“All right,” the man said, wide eyes fixed on Turk. “We get it. Call him off.”

Michael hesitated just a half-second. Then he said, “Easy, Turk. Come on back.”

Turk backed off and stopped growling, but never took his eyes off of the man as he trotted back to Michael.

“Well,” the woman said, “He’s got the spirit, that’s for sure. How many fights has he had?”

“Good fights or crapshows that didn’t even last thirty seconds?” Michael asked.

“Easy, Michael,” Faith said in his earpiece. “Don’t lay it on too thick.”

Sure enough, one of the men narrowed his eyes and leaned forward. “You have your dog,” he said, “We all have handguns. Not to mention thirty men outside with more guns. Show some respect.”

Michael lifted his hands and said, “No disrespect intended. He’s had seventeen fights. Most of them ended within a minute. The only time he had trouble was a Tibetan Mastiff some visiting Yakuza brought. Took him almost three minutes to break the mastiff’s neck.”

Michael’s stomach turned as he thought of the fights he had just seen. God, he hated this.

The woman chuckled. “A part of me still thinks you’re lying to us,” she said, “but we’ll give you a shot. Actually, Roman here has a dog he wants to try.”

The man Turk had threatened narrowed his eyes. “You sure you want to lose Turk that fast?”

Michael grinned humorlessly. “No disrespect intended,” he said, “but Turk will utterly obliterate your dog. Whatever it is.”

Roman glared and said, “You talk a lot of shit, white boy. Maybe I should throw you and your dog in with Ceasar.”

“Calm down, Roman,” one of the other men said, “he’s just backing up his dog. You sure got a lot of faith in that little shepherd. You have other dogs?”

“A few,” Michael said, “I had more, but I made the mistake of letting them eat dinner together. I learned that lesson the hard way.”

“Let me guess,” Roman said sarcastically, “Turk killed them all?”

Michael grinned again. “All of your doubts will be erased when Turk makes Ceasar bleed out just like his namesake.”

Roman glared at him and said, “Maybe you and me will go after the dogs go.”

If only I were so lucky, Michael thought.

“You’ll have to forgive Roman,” one of the other men said, “He’s still pissed that Franco got eaten alive by that pitbull.”

The three others laughed. Roman continued to glare at Michael.

“Hey, didn’t Vinny find that dog?” the woman asked.

Michael forced himself not to react.

“Yeah, he did. He was really proud of himself, too. That was the last dog he picked up for us, huh?"

“Yeah. That was Vinny.”

Well, well, Michael thought. *So Roman lost a fight because of a dog Vincent Mariano found.*

In his earpiece, Faith said, “Got it, Michael. That our guy?”

“Yeah?” Michael said, answering Faith’s question and framing it as a question for the benefit of the gangsters. “What happened to them?”

“Someone killed them,” one of the other men said, “bad. Hey, that wasn’t you, was it, Roman?”

Roman sneered, and in his earpiece, Michael heard Faith say, “Two minutes, Michael. When you hear us get inside, act like you’re running away with the gangsters. Then find us. We have your handgun and fifteen officers that Garvey assures me will be more than enough for thirty gangsters.”

Michael really hoped it didn’t come to shooting, but it was nice to know that if it did, he’d be able to participate. “All right, boys,” he said, “let’s talk business.”

***

Faith heard a yelp of pain and a cheer as she and Garvey burst into the warehouse. She had just enough time to see a surprised Rottweiler lift its head from the corpse of a pitbull before the officers on the other end of the warehouse started firing.

It was a perfect raid. Most of the outlaws scattered, never even thinking about their weapons.

But a few did, and as Faith's luck would have it, they were on her side of the warehouse. She and Garvey dove behind some crates that served as makeshift bleachers and fired back at a half dozen gangsters who, like so many did, somehow felt that holding their guns sideways would make them more deadly.

Fortunately, all it did was make them less accurate, allowing Faith to subdue them without having to kill them. She and Garvey rushed forward and Garvey pointed her own handgun at the wounded gangsters and warned, "I'm Satan with a sunburn compared to her, and I can't aim for crap, so if you decide to get stupid and fight me, I'll just aim for the chest and keep firing until you stop moving, *capisce?"*

Faith left her and moved across the warehouse. A few other groups of criminals had found cover and were engaging with the officers. Faith's path brought her to a group of four officers engaging with seven such criminals.

She looked around wildly for Michael and Turk as she took cover and returned fire. They were nowhere in sight.

"Come on, Michael," she said, "For Heaven's sake, hurry up."

One of the gangsters lifted himself above his cover and aimed his weapon squarely at her. She fired once, the bullet impacting his shoulder and sending him spinning to the ground with a cry of anguish.

The other criminals dropped their weapons and lifted their hands. Faith left them in the care of the officers and moved on.

She saw Turk and Michael then, running vaguely in their direction while trying to make it look like they were running away. When they drew close, they veered directly toward Faith. One of the gangsters shouted and pointed, and Faith had enough time to see three men and a woman turn to Michael in shock. They glared, and Faith realized those were the organizers."

"Roman is the one who looks like a bodybuilder."

Faith identified him and radioed Garvey. "Michael and I are going after the suspect. Have your officers cover us."

She handed Michael his gun, and the two of them ran after Roman, who glared at them a moment before turning to run.

Too long a moment. Turk caught him before he made it five steps. Roman had seen what Turk was capable of during the meeting with Michael, so he didn't even try to resist. Fear replaced the anger in his face. He lifted his hands and said in a high-pitched voice that was utterly incongruous for a man his size, "Please don't hurt me! I surrender!"

"On the ground!" Faith called, keeping her weapon trained on him.

He complied, and Michael stepped forward to cuff him. Once the cuffs were on, Faith called Turk to her side. A flash of anger returned to Roman's face. "You're a coward, Mike. If that's even your real name."

"It's my name," Michael said, hauling him to his feet, "and if it helps you feel better, you can call me whatever you want. In the meantime, you're under arrest for cruelty to animals, running an illegal gambling operation, and a lot of other charges I can't think of off the top of my head. Oh yeah, and we suspect you of murdering Harvey Harris and Vincent Mariano."

Roman, showing a touch of foresight for a change, clammed up.

CHAPTER THIRTEEN

The Wolfman parked his truck across the street and shut off the lights. In the city, he would never have been able to get away with that, but in the suburbs, people never imagined that anything bad would happen. They were safe in their own little bubble, and the bad things happened to Other People.

Well, everyone was Other People until they weren't. He had learned that the hard way.

He checked his tools and confirmed that they were in running shape. The electric portion of the collar was the electrode from a cattle prod, a radio receiver and a mechanism for limiting the amperage of the shock so he could adjust the current via a modified RC controller. It was a crude looking and rather ugly weapon, but it was effective, and he knew from experience that function was more important than form. Besides, the weapon was unique and, therefore, virtually untraceable as long as he didn't leave anything behind.

He never left anything behind. Nothing that mattered anyway. The boots he wore were probably the most common pair of work boots in the country. Hundreds of pairs were sold every week, even in his large size. They wouldn't be able to track him by his bootprints. He wore gloves and an equally common type of jeans and t-shirt, all bargain basement, all worn by millions of people.

Of course, he left the bodies behind, but that was good. People should see what these men were.

He got out of his car and headed to the house. Today, in addition to his normal clothing and his wolf mask, he wore a hooded sweatshirt, oversized and baggy to give the impression that he was heavier than he was. It was a thin disguise. If anyone did happen to see him, they could give the police a fairly accurate description of his height and gender, but once more, he wasn't all that uncommon. He was a big man, but not so big that he would turn heads.

He knocked on the door. A few seconds later, the homeowner answered because, of course, he did. It was the suburbs. If someone was knocking on his door late at night, it surely was something innocuous like a need for directions or to borrow a phone. No one actually killed people in their own homes.

The homeowner really should have known better, considering the people he ran with, but stupidity abounded.

"Can I help you?" the man asked. Then he saw the mask, and his eyes widened.

The Wolfman shoved hard. The man fell back with a cry, and the Wolfman quickly and calmly stepped inside and shut and locked the door.

"Hey," the homeowner said in a shaky voice. "Hey, I have money in a safe upstairs. I can get it for you. Please don't hurt me."

"You have a gun in the safe upstairs too, Bobby," the Wolfman said. "I'm pretty sure that'll hurt me if I let you use it."

The homeowner, Robert "Bobby" Evans, blinked in surprise. "How do you know my name?"

"Do you remember Fluffy Face?" the Wolfman asked, setting his bag carefully on the floor. Harry started to get up, and in a swift motion, the Wolfman stepped forward and kicked him back to the floor. "Stay still, please," he commanded.

"Fluffy Face?" Bobby said. "What the fuck are you talking about?"

"That's the name Jeanie Peterson gave to her pet Wolfhound. Fluffy Face. She called him that because Fluffy Face liked to give her butterfly kisses when she was sad, and his whiskers felt fluffy. She loved that dog, you know."

Bobby looked confused for a moment longer. Then his eyes widened in understanding. "Hey, look, I was just doing a job."

"You can't possibly be so foolish as to think that's an excuse," the Wolfman said, retrieving the collar.

Bobby saw the crude electric mechanism and paled. A stain formed on the front of his pants. Normally, that didn't happen until after the Wolfman started. It seemed Bobby was even more of a coward than the other thief.

"Look, I'm sorry," Bobby said, "I was scared. They're dangerous guys, you know. You can't say no to them."

"Of course you can," the Wolfman said, flipping the shock collar on. "There's always a choice. Besides," he started toward Bobby, "Harvey Harris didn't threaten you. He sent one of his whores to butter you up. And when he suggested to you there was more where that came from, well—" He leaned down, "you just couldn't resist, could you."

Bobby cried out and slapped at the collar, knocking it out of the Wolfman's hands. He scrambled backwards and tried to get to his feet, but the Wolfman was faster. He slammed his fist into Bobby's temple, knocking the man out cold.

He got up and retrieved the collar, then set it carefully around Bobby's neck. He cinched it tight, and the cold pressure of the spikes woke Bobby. He groaned, and the Wolfman rolled him over. "Please," Bobby said, "please don't."

"You sent Fluffy Face to die," the Wolfman said, "now I'm going to return the favor."

"Please!"

The Wolfman pressed the switch.

CHAPTER FOURTEEN

Garvey was in a wonderful mood as she and her officers booked the arrested gangsters. “This is the single biggest blow we’ve dealt to the Georgia Syndicate since I started with the department,” she said to the agents with a grin. “Aside from the dogfighting, we’ve arrested most of Harris’s old muscle, and Mr. Kerry is known as one of the go-to people for drug running in the state. He is to drugs what Harris was to prostitution."

“Congratulations,” Michael said with a haunted smile.

Faith’s heart went out to him. She hadn’t had a chance to talk to him about what he witnessed at the warehouse, but from the brief glimpse she had scene, it couldn’t have been pretty. In hindsight, it was a good thing she hadn’t gone in. She didn’t think she would have been able to keep her cool the way Michael did.

“Speaking of Mr. Kerry,” Garvey said, “he’s ready for you now. We have him in room three. I don’t know if you’ll get much from him, though. He knows better than to speak against the Syndicate.”

“I don’t need him to rat out his gang,” Faith said, “I just need to know if he’s our killer.”

“Well,” Garvey said, “good luck to you. Either way, he’s going to jail for a long time. Maybe you can use that. I’m pretty sure the DA will cut him a deal if he can tell us who the killer is. Of course, if *he’s* the killer, that won’t work, but it’s always worth a shot.”

“We’ll see what we can do,” Faith said.

She, Michael, and Turk headed to interrogation room three. Roman Kerry was shackled to the floor, the chair and the table. No one was taking any chances with him, considering his size and obvious temper. He glared at the agents when they walked in and said, "So the coward has to tie me up to talk to me."

“If it helps you to think that way about it,” Michael said.

“Yeah, you’re so above it all, aren’t you?” Roman said, “You’re so much better than all of us lowly street types.”

“If you want to get into a pissing match with me, you can do it after we talk,” Michael said.

“I’m not talking to you,” Roman said.

“Not even if I use the word deal?” Michael asked.

Roman laughed. “Did that pretty little cop tell you they were gonna offer me a deal? No one’s giving me a deal, man. That’s just something cops say.”

“Well, we’re FBI,” Faith said, “We outrank the cops. If we say you get a deal, then you get a deal.”

"And I should trust you? You got me here because you lied to me. And hey, good job. The game recognizes the game. You got me. But I'm not going to help you get anyone else. Even if I was a snitch, talking to you only gets me killed, inside or outside."

“Well, how about this, then?” Faith said, “You don’t have to talk about anyone else. You tell us what you know about the deaths of Harvey Harris and Vincent Mariano. You tell us where to find the evidence we need, and as far as the world knows, we just figured it out ourselves.”

Roman shook his head incredulously at the agents. “All right,” he said. “If you two just need to hear the sounds of your own voices a bit, go ahead and keep talking, but this is it for me.”

“What do you think will happen when your bosses find out that you just screwed up an entire dogfighting ring because you got stupid?” Faith asked. “Not to mention that without Harris, they don’t have prostitution and without you, they don’t have drugs?”

Roman sat silently, staring contemptuously at the officers.

Faith looked down at Turk. She mouthed, "Be mean."

Turk lunged at Roman, snapping and barking in front of his face, glaring and snarling. The criminal paled a few shades but remained silent, even when Turk leaned forward so close their noses were almost touching.

Faith sighed and called Turk back. She and Michael tried different tacks for a half hour or so, but eventually, they had to accept that they weren’t going to be able to get him to talk. They left and met with Garvey behind the two-way mirror. Garvey nodded sympathetically. “Yeah, the street boys will usually break if you lean on ‘em hard enough, but when you get into management, it gets harder to get them to talk. The thing is, Roman's not wrong. His superiors *will* kill him if he talks. Even if he takes full responsibility for the murders, unless he does it with their permission, they’ll waste him.”

“Have you learned anything from the others?” Faith asked.

“Well, that pitbull the other organizers were talking about,” Garvey said, “Apparently, Roman killed it in front of people. Tied him to a stake and shot him, then gave a speech about not messing with his money. Typical tough guy crap. But we have him for animal cruelty, operating a gambling business without a gambling license or a business license, endangerment, and a bunch of minor charges. We'll almost certainly get solicitation to stick too. Not sure about the drugs. People at his level usually make sure nothing's traceable to them, but we have enough to put him in jail for fifteen years, at least."

"All right," Faith said, "we're going to go get some coffee. If by some miracle he does happen to talk, come get us."

"Will do," Garvey said, "I wouldn't hold your breath, though."

Faith and Michael headed to the breakroom. The coffee was of the sort that Michael would derisively call "hotel coffee," but when Faith handed him a cup, he drank it down in three big gulps, undeterred by the heat or the flavor.

Faith poured him another cup and sat across from him. He stared ahead, his eyes spacy. "Hey," she said softly, placing a hand over his. "You okay?"

He took a deep breath and released it slowly. "I figured out why they wanted Macy."

"Bait dog?"

He nodded. "I don't get people sometimes, man." He chuckled. "I don't even get myself. I mean, I've hunted plenty of people who killed other people, but I've never hated anyone as much as I hated Gaucho and Roman. Everyone there, really. I don't know why, but something about watching the dogfights just seemed worse than anything I've ever witnessed."

Faith nodded. "It's the same reason why people who hurt children are worse to us than people who hurt adults. We see dogs as defenseless." She looked at Turk, who had taken the opportunity to nap for a moment. "Even when they're not, they're just so dependent on us that when people take advantage of that, it just enrages us. There's an unwritten rule we have that you don't attack people who can't defend themselves."

"Yeah," Michael said. "Well, bottom line, I can't wait to get home, and next time, organized crime can handle this. Give me my garden variety homicidal psychopaths over this crap any day."

Faith smiled sadly and squeezed his hand.

The door flew open, and Garvey leaned in, her face deadly serious.

"He talked?" Faith asked hopefully.

Garvey shook her head. "No, but he's not the murderer."

"How do you…" then Faith understood.

***

"Robert Evans," Garvey said. "Forty-three, divorced, lived alone. Looks like a home invasion. The killer forced his way inside, overpowered Evans, slipped the collar on, and… well, you can see the rest."

Evans was in even worse shape than the previous two victims. His body was contorted, his limbs pulled into a fetal position, hands claws and face a rictus of pain. His eyes were glassy and shrunken, an effect of the electricity burning the fluid off. He looked like a horror movie.

"This guy's escalating," Michael said, "the next one's going to look like a burnt hot dog."

Faith couldn't think of anything to say to that. She asked Garvey, "What's the time of death?"

"Coroner says between two and four hours ago."

In other words, when they raided the warehouse. Roman Kerry couldn't possibly be their killer.

Faith sighed. "Did the neighbors see anything?"

Garvey shook her head. "This is one of those neighborhoods where people go to bed at ten o'clock and don't turn their lights on until seven. Everyone minds their own business because everyone assumes no one else has any business *to* mind. I'm pretty sure this is the first murder this neighborhood has ever seen."

"Then who placed the call?"

"Security patrol. He noticed the front door ajar, and when he went in to check, he found Robert. His supervisor confirms he left dispatch twenty minutes before arriving, so no chance he's the killer."

"Dis Evans own a dog?"

"No. Never has. No connection to the dogfighting ring or the Syndicate in any way."

Faith shook her head. "So why?"

They fell silent. Turk started sniffing around the body, looking for anything that would connect this victim to the previous ones. Other than bootprints that matched the one at the second crime scene, he found nothing.

"So no one saw or heard any vehicles?" Faith asked, "no lights? Nothing?"

“If they did, then they didn’t consider it out of the ordinary or important enough to mention,” Garvey said.

“So why him?” Faith asked again. “Why any of them? I get the gang connection between Harris and Mariano, but why Evans? The man lives fifteen miles from anywhere the gang operates.”

“Maybe he hurt one of the girls at a club,” Michael suggested. “You said he was divorced? Maybe we should talk to his ex-wife. Maybe he was abusive, and he screwed with the wrong girl.”

“If that’s the case, then we’re looking at a gang hit,” Faith said, “and then I have to wonder why the Syndicate would kill one of their street bosses without a replacement ready.”

“Maybe it wasn’t one of the Syndicate’s girls. Iliev told us that the Syndicate controls all of the prostitution in Atlanta. Maybe the Bulgarians moved their operation to the suburbs.”

“Maybe,” Faith said, “but why kill a john like this? I could see killing Harris this way to send a message, but a civilian? That’s a lot of risk just to kill a nobody.”

“Well,” Michael said, “it paid off.”

Faith supposed he had a point.

“I want to talk with forensics,” she told Garvey. “Maybe they have details that can help us narrow down our source.”

“Be my guest,” Garvey said.

The CSI in charge was a bespectacled man around Faith’s age named Guillaume. “But you can call me Gil.”

“Well, Gil, what can you tell us?” Michael asked.

“Well,” Gil said, “Cause of death is pretty obvious.” He pointed to a livid red wound that encircled Evans’ neck. A pool of drying blood had settled underneath the wound. “He was shocked so bad that the skin of his neck literally melted onto the collar. The killer took a souvenir home with him.”

Turk sniffed at the wound to get the scent, staying a respectful distance away so he didn’t compromise the evidence. Faith asked, “Can you tell us anything about the weapon? Any guess on the kind of model?”

“That is beyond my area of expertise,” Gil said, “but I don’t know if it would help you to know exactly what model it is. Those things aren’t tracked by serial number, and even if they were, well, Atlanta’s a big city. It’s a pretty good bet that there are thousands of those things out here.”

"What about the electricity?" Michael asked. "How was that provided?"

"Well, we're looking at something in the range of one hundred twenty milliamps, give or take. That's definitely enough to kill someone, but depending on the voltage you use, it might not kill them right away."

"So he's torturing his victims."

"Oh yeah. Evans here probably took over a minute to lose consciousness and another minute to die. Then our bad guy kept going for… I'd guess another two or three minutes to turn him into jerky." He grimaced. "Sorry. That was uncalled for."

It was, but Faith wasn't concerned with Gil's propriety at the moment. "Any other physical evidence? Fibers, body fluids?"

"No body fluids," Gil replied, "a few fibers. We'll run them at the lab, but I can tell you just from a cursory examination that they're going to come back as twenty-dollar pants and a ten-dollar t-shirt. Once more, the kind of stuff that half the city wears."

Faith and Michael looked at each other. "Thank you, Gil," Michael said. "If you find anything else, please call us."

"Will do."

They stepped away, and Faith said, "So our killer is taking care only to cover his fingerprints but not bothering with the rest of the evidence because it's so commonplace that it might as well be untraceable."

"Hiding in plain sight," Michael said. "Came in through the front door and everything."

"But he's not careless," Faith said, "because he takes everything with him, and covers his fingerprints, which is the only thing he could leave behind that could identify *him* and not everyone in Georgia."

"So are we thinking law enforcement?" Michael asked, "someone who would know enough to understand what's worth hiding and what isn't?"

"It's possible," Faith said, "it's also possible he just knows very *little* about crime scene investigation and just didn't think to cover his boots in plastic or wear clothing that wouldn't fray."

"So we're surrounded by a sea of possibilities, none of which leads to certainty," Michael summarized.

"One of them leads to certainty," Faith said. "We just have to figure out which one. I want to talk to the ex-wife. Maybe she'll be more willing to talk about what her husband was into than the gang is willing to talk about what they're into."

"It's certainly worth a shot," Michael agreed.

CHAPTER FIFTEEN

"Dammit. That stupid asshole."

Laura Hagerty chose to go by her maiden name. She lived in Marietta, a half hour northwest of Atlanta and a forty-five-minute drive from her husband's home. Faith and Michael arrived just as the sun poked its gaze over the horizon.She had answered the door wearing only a bathrobe, and that, accompanied with the eye roll and the lack of any visible sign of grief gave Faith and Michael pause.

"All right," Laura said. "Come on inside. You can make yourselves coffee if you want. The stuff's on the counter. I'm going to go get dressed and tell my boss that I can't come in today. After that, I'm all yours."

She headed upstairs and Michael and Faith stepped inside, Turk following. Turk sniffed around, trying to find a scent that matched what he'd detected from the crime scene. He didn't get anything. Apparently, it had been a while since Mr. Evans and Ms. Hagerty had seen each other.

The house itself was stylish and well-decorated. The furniture was high quality, and the appliances were top-of-the-line models. It was noticeably nicer than the furnishings at Evans' house.

"I guess we know who 'won' the divorce," Michael quipped.

Laura came downstairs a moment later in a t-shirt and sweatpants. Her expression betrayed no grief, only irritation. "I'm gonna need to cancel my vacation," she said, "I was really counting on next month's alimony payment. Hey, do either of you know how to petition the court for a judgment on his assets?"

"We don't," Faith said, "that's not what we're here for."

"Well, what are you here for?"

"To find out who murdered your ex-husband."

Laura paused. "Ah," she said, her voice much more subdued. "I didn't realize he was murdered."

"We hadn't mentioned it yet," Michael said.

"Am I… do I need a lawyer?" Laura asked.

"Not at this time," Faith said. "We don't suspect you of being involved."

Indeed, Faith found it difficult to imagine the five-foot-one, hundred-pound Laura of killing three grown men, especially in that manner. She definitely didn't overcome Harvey Harris in a fistfight before murdering him. It was an outside possibility, she supposed, that Laura could have paid someone to murder the three men, but Faith didn't think that was likely, and if it was, she didn't want Laura to think they thought it was likely. Not yet, anyway.

"Got it," Laura said. "That's good. Do you mind if I smoke?"

Faith gestured for her to go ahead. Laura walked to the kitchen and pulled a pack of cigarettes and a lighter from one of the drawers. Faith noticed her hands were trembling. "Is everything all right, Ms. Hagerty."

"Please, call me Laura," Laura said, lighting her cigarette. "I hate that name, Hagerty. It sounds like hag and haggard, and I left Bobby to try to put both off as long as possible."

"But you still went back to your maiden name," Michael pointed out.

"Yeah, well," she took another drag. "I guess I hated Bobby more."

"Enough to kill him?" Faith asked.

Laura met her eyes. "I thought you said I don't need a lawyer."

"I'm pretty sure you don't," Faith said, "but since this is a murder investigation, and you did say you hated our victim, I have to ask."

Laura scoffed. "Well, to answer your first question, no, everything is not all right. You might think me a gold-digger for saying this, but I've been living primarily off of Bobby's alimony for the past seven years. If I don't get at least some of his assets, then I'm royally screwed. I'll have to sell my house and end up living in a crappy apartment on Hansen Street again."

Faith's ears perked up at the mention of Hansen Street. "When did you move out of Hansen Street?"

"When Bobby married me fifteen years ago," she said, "back when I was a naïve twenty-four-year-old and having a man who could do passably well in bed was all that mattered to me." She chuckled. "Silly little me, I never considered that a man who was good in bed might be good to other women too."

"When you lived on Hansen Street," Faith said, "did you have any interactions with the Georgia Syndicate?"

"The who now?"

"Did you ever run into trouble with any of the street gangs?"

She chuckled. “The gangs? No. I made sure I was inside with my doors and windows locked and my gun loaded. I kept waiting for someone to try to convince me to work at one of the clubs, but no one did. I guess I wasn’t as pretty as I thought I was.”

In Faith’s opinion, Laura would be a very handsome woman if she smiled more and was no doubt breathtaking, not to mention the petite figure that so many men preferred.

Then again, it was easier to work with willing women than to force unwilling women, and the Syndicate was seemingly very concerned with minimizing trouble. Faith wouldn't be surprised to read about Roman Kerry having an accident in prison, whether he talked or not. The other organizers had gotten away, meaning leadership would hear that it was entirely Roman's fault.

“When did you and your husband divorce?” Michael asked.

She smiled slightly. “You really need to know all that?”

“You can assume we need the answers to every question we ask,” Faith replied.

“All right,” Laura said, lifting her hands placatingly. “I was just asking. Well, like I said earlier, I’ve been living off of alimony for seven years, so that’s when I left him. I caught him with one of my coworkers. It was the eighth time he’d cheated on me in eight years, and that’s only the women I know about.”

She took another drag on the cigarette. “The crazy thing is that I didn’t mind that he ran around with other women. Not all that much, anyway. I get that men need a lot more sex than most women do, and I’ll admit I was never a ‘freak in the sheets.’ If he had kept it quiet and away from our house, I would have been perfectly content to look the other way a few days a month.” She took another drag. “But I draw the line at being treated with no respect. I told him we were through, and he… do you need details on the divorce?”

“If you think they’re relevant.”

“Well, I don’t think any of this is relevant,” Laura said, “but I’ll just leave it at this: he was very confident that I wouldn’t win the judgment that I, of course, ended up winning. He fought the judgment until the court ordered him to pay up or sell his house and give me half.”

"Did you have any contact with him after the divorce?"

She shook her head. “He tried to come over about six months after we split. He was drunk and wanted to have sex. I told him to get lost and find one of his whores. After that, he just sent the checks, and I just cashed them.”

She looked at Faith's expression and smiled slightly. "You think I'm a special sort of evil, don't you, for talking about a dead man like this."

"My standards of evil are very different from yours, I'm sure," Faith replied.

Laura chuckled. "Yeah, I guess that makes sense. Well, I don't know what else I can tell you. I figured he would get himself killed sooner or later, so I guess I just dealt with those emotions a while ago."

"Why did you feel he would get himself killed?"

Laura paused with her cigarette halfway to her lips. She frowned slightly, then finished the drag. She tapped the ashes directly onto the table and said, "Well, he was involved in… something. I don't know exactly what, but I know that I didn't want to be involved in it."

"But it didn't have anything to do with your divorce?"

"You'd think it would, wouldn't you?" Laura said with bitter sarcasm.

She lifted her cigarette again and found it was spent. She returned to the kitchen and got another cigarette. She lit it and took a drag, then said, "No. I just looked the other way. I was really good at doing that. I think that's why it pissed me off so much that he had eight women in our house. I mean, for Christ's sake, spend fifty bucks on a motel room and wear a condom."

"Are you familiar with the name Harvey Harris?"

She shook her head. "No, I don't know that name. Is he a suspect?"

"No, he's another victim."

Laura's eyes widened in shock. "You mean there's more than one murder?"

"Three so far," Faith confirmed. "Vincent Mariano, Harvey Harris, and your ex-husband."

She watched Laura carefully as she mentioned the names. Laura showed no sign of recognition.

"Jesus," Laura said, "am I in danger?"

"That depends," Faith said, "are you familiar with Roman Kerry?"

Laura flinched and paled considerably. "Roman Kerry?"

Michael leaned forward and said, "This is when you might need a lawyer."

"No, no," Laura said, shaking her head. "No, I didn't have anything to do with Roman Kerry."

"But you know the name," Faith said.

“Yes, I…” Laura sighed and took a deep drag on her cigarette. “I…” she sighed. “Okay, I lied earlier when I said that I hadn’t seen Bobby in years. I…” she slumped. “I went over last month.”

“Why?”

She met Faith’s eyes and said, “Well, it turns out that finding men who do passably well in bed is not as easy as you’d think.”

“So you went over for sex?”

Laura lifted her hand and let it drop. “Yeah. It had been nine months since I… well, you don’t need the gruesome details. Yes, I called him and asked him if he wanted to get laid. I don’t know that a man’s ever lived who’s answered no to that question. So I went over, we…” she shrugged bitterly. “…did it, and while I was lying in bed after, I overheard him on the phone with a man named Roman Kerry.”

“What did you hear?”

“Not much. Bobby just kept reassuring him that he would fix it. He didn’t need to send anyone over, Bobby would take care of it.”

“Did you ask him what he meant by that?”

She shook her head. “I asked him who was on the phone, and he just said he had made some powerful new friends who needed a favor from him.”

“You didn’t ask who his powerful new friends might be?”

“Hell no. I went home as soon as I could.”

“So you never saw Roman Kerry personally.”

“No, and I don’t want to.” She took another drag and said, “Look, agent, Bobby was many things, but he wasn’t a coward. So when I tell you that he looked pale as a ghost after talking to Roman, you know I mean something serious.”

“Very serious,” Faith said, “Roman Kerry is a high-ranking member of the Georgia Syndicate.”

“Is that like the mob?”

“More or less,” Faith confirmed.

Laura scoffed and shook her head. “Figures. Of course, Bobby would do something stupid like that. Well, I'm glad that's the last time I saw him." She shook her head again. "That stupid son of a bitch."

“And you never talked to him in any way?”

“I keep saying no,” Laura replied, “and you keep asking. That means you don’t believe me. Why?”

“I don’t disbelieve you,” Faith said, “but I have Roman Kerry in custody, and I will be asking him if he knows you.”

Laura paled. “I don’t suppose you could avoid that?” she said, “I really don’t know him, and I don’t want a target on my back.”

“If you have a target on your back,” Faith said, “it won’t have anything to do with Roman.”

CHAPTER SIXTEEN

Roman Kerry rubbed sleep from his eyes as he sat down in the chair across from the officers. Two armed officers stood behind him in case he decided to get stupid. "Well, look who came to visit," he said groggily. "Did you miss me?"

"Laura Evans," Faith said.

"What?"

"You might know her as Laura Hagerty?"

"Except I don't. Who is Laura Hagerty?"

"The ex-wife of Robert Evans."

"You might know him as Bobby," Michael added.

Roman's eyes widened. He might not know Laura, but he definitely knew Bobby. He caught himself and turned his face to stone.

"Before you decide not to talk," Faith said, "Let me paint you a picture. First, we know you're not the killer. That's pretty obvious, because we found Bobby Evans dead earlier this morning."

Roman's face flickered in surprise.

"So that's good news for you," Faith continued, "and here's why you want to help us find his killer. Right now, the Syndicate is going to be pissed. They've just lost three very important revenue streams in the Atlanta region because someone decided to turn into a slasher horror star and brought a lot of heat on their operations here. That someone is still out there causing trouble.

"Now, as it stands at the moment, they're going to want someone to answer for that, and you are, if you'll permit the irony, the biggest dog in the kennel. Frankly, whether you talk or not, I wouldn't give you very long to live."

Roman's eyes flickered again, and his shoulders slumped slightly.

"But," Faith continued, "if you help us out and as a result, we find the person who *is* responsible for all of this, we cut a deal. We can't make all of the charges go away, but we can make a lot of them go away. Suddenly, fifteen years turns into five, out in two if you behave yourself. And, we let it slip that a source within the gang gave us the information we needed to stop this murderer, so your bosses deduce that you helped put a stop to it. Maybe you don't get to be management anymore. Maybe that's not enough for you to keep your job. But even criminals have some standards. I'd be willing to bet you can keep your life."

Roman was silent for a long moment, but Faith could see in his eyes that he was breaking, so she didn't press further. Finally, he sighed and slumped. "All right," he said, "you can really help with the charges?"

"You give us our killer, we do everything we can to make this easier on you," Faith confirmed.

"Okay," Roman said, "Yeah. I knew Bobby."

Bingo.

"How?" Faith asked.

Roman shrugged. "It's good to have someone clean to work with. Someone who won't have a record pop up if a cop pulls him over. I always told Harris that Vinny was a bad bet. He had a past with the mob in Boston, not much, but enough that if *he* ran a stop sign, a lot of priors were going to show up. Me? I looked for civilians."

"Where did you find Bobby?"

"At a club. Harris ran sex in Atlanta, but a lot of us had fingers in the pie. I kept my eye out for someone divorced, older but not too old and overconfident who didn't have a record. You'd be amazed what guys will do for a young woman who won't say no."

Try me, Faith thought.

"So you found Bobby," Michael said, "what did Bobby do for you?"

"Whatever I needed him to do. Nothing too crazy. It wouldn't help me out if I ended up giving him a record. I just had him run errands."

"Give me an example of an errand."

"Well, I had him pick stuff up for me. Dogs, usually."

"You didn't want him to have a criminal record, so you hired him to steal dogs?" Faith said incredulously.

Roman chuckled mirthlessly. "It's a lot easier to steal things than you'd think, agent," he said, "Yeah, I had him pick up dogs. He actually got Franco." Roman nodded at Michael. "That was my champion dog until Vinny found that pit bull. Big dog. Wolfhound. I gave him a bonus for that."

"Who did he steal Franco from?"

Roman shrugged. "I didn't need to know, so I didn't ask. It helps to know as little as possible in this business, agent. That's why a guy like Vinny can work fifteen years for the mob and get off with a slap on the wrist, but a guy like me runs a few things for a few years, and the best the FBI can do is a reduced prison sentence and a felony record."

"So Bobby never mentioned anything about where he got the dogs?"

"I made sure he didn't. My exact words to him were, 'I want the product to show up under my tree like Santa Claus, you feel me? I don't want a shipping label, a return address or a collar. As far as I'll ever know, the Lord just blessed me. Got it?' He got it."

Faith and Michael shared a look, then stood. "Thank you for your time, Mr. Kerry. We'll see what we can do about your charges."

***

The original home of Franco the Wolfhound turned out to be harder to find than Faith expected. No shelters reported any Wolfhounds found within the past six months, and there was no police report filed.

"We only take those reports if the dog is registered," Garvey explained. "There's no other way to know for sure that the dogs actually belong to their owner. It amazes me how many owners don't want to spend the thirty bucks and the hour of time to get the dog registered and inspected."

"I've learned that most people are convinced that bad things only happen to other people," Faith said.

Garvey shook her head. "How many people need to die for us to get over that idiocy?"

Faith chose not to comment on that. She and Michael browsed through local listings and social media clubs and finally found something.

The Wolfhound's name wasn't Franco originally. Fluffy Face was a six-year-old Irish Wolfhound who, like most members of his breed, was absolutely enormous. He was listed at three feet at the shoulder and a massive one hundred eighty-eight pounds. That made him over twice as big as Turk and half again as big as the largest Rottweilers. No wonder he had been a champion fighting dog.

The picture posted of him on the social media page of Atlanta Dog Lovers didn't look like a fighting dog. He was smiling the wide grin that Faith saw anytime Turk was in an especially good mood and seemed utterly devoted to a little girl who hugged him tightly.

The post was from two months ago, and it broke Faith's heart. The owner, Donald Peterson, begged for information on Fluffy Face, his granddaughter's dog. Fluffy Face was as gentle and loving—the post said—as his name suggested. Jeanie, the granddaughter, hadn't stopped crying for him. Any information would be met with a reward.

Faith doubted the information they had to share would be met with a reward. She sighed and wiped her hand across her eyes.

"Assholes," Michael said viciously. "God, I wish I could feed them all to the dogs they abuse."

"Yeah," Faith said, "I'm right there with you."

The page listed an address a few miles from the station. Faith and Michael headed there with Turk, who seemed alternately more subdued and more restless than usual. Faith wondered if he knew that they were hunting people who hurt dogs. She thought of Turk, so recently lost and in the clutches of a sadistic serial killer. She recalled the joy and relief she felt when he returned safely to her. She could easily imagine how her heart would break if he had been found dead.

This was going to hurt.

They reached Donald Peterson's house just after lunchtime. School was still in session, so at least they didn't need to worry about Jeanie finding out.

Donald Peterson opened the door, and the look on his face when he saw the officers pierced Faith to her core. He sighed and slumped forward, looking every bit the old man he was. "Well," he said, "the FBI is here. Either that means you found my anti-war letters from Vietnam, or you found my dog somewhere he shouldn't be."

Faith lifted an eyebrow. "You're aware of the dog fighting ring?"

"I'm aware of dog fighting rings in general," Donald said, "I don't know about any of them, but when Fluffy didn't come home and no one managed to see a two-hundred-pound dog, I figured someone picked him up for no good reason." He shook his head. "Well, come on in."

The agents followed him inside. Turk walked straight to Donald's side, looking up at him with big, sympathetic eyes. Donald smiled down at him and reached down to ruffle his fur. "Dogs are wonderful, aren't they?" he said.

"Yes," Faith agreed. "I'm so sorry about yours."

Donald sighed. "I'm more worried about Jeanie. She's only six years old. She's going to just be devastated. I'm not gonna tell her what happened, obviously, but I'll have to tell her that he's gone for good. She still prays every night for God to bring him home safely."

He slumped into his easy chair and buried his head in his hands. Faith and Michael sat on the couch and waited for him to look up. "I'll get her a new dog," he said, "I know a guy who breeds Wolfhounds. I'll find a puppy for her, and we'll do it right this time. I'll register it, I'll build a better fence and keep it locked. I'll… hell, I'll buy a gun if I have to. Christ."

He pressed his hands to his face again, and Faith could see his lower lip trembling.

"When did Fluffy go missing?" Faith asked.

"Two months ago," Donald said, confirming the evidence from Laura Hagerty and the online post. "We came home one day, and the backyard gate was opened and Fluffy was gone. We thought he had got out to chase a squirrel, so we just put his food out and waited for him to come home. When he didn't, we called the police, but the police said they couldn't help unless he was registered." He sighed. "So, we did it the old-fashioned way. I guess the online ads were new-fashioned, but you know what I mean. Dammit, I knew he was gone. I told Jeanie that he was probably just lost, and if we prayed hard enough, he'd find his way home. I guess I hoped he would."

"Mr. Peterson, did you ever meet a man named Robert Evans?"

"Evans? No. Is he the man who took my dog?"

"Yes," Faith confirmed.

Donald's eyes went dark. "Is he here?"

"No," Faith replied. "He was murdered last night."

"Hmm," Donald huffed. "Well, I hope you won't think too poorly of me if I say I'm not sorry. Do you need me to confirm my whereabouts?"

Faith looked at the old and frail Donald and shook her head. "No, we don't suspect you. However, I do want to know if you can think of anyone else who would have wanted to get revenge for Fluffy."

Donald chuckled. "Well, most people I know would be pissed off about anyone stealing a dog, but enough to do something about it? No. Hell, even if I could, I don't know that I would put myself or my granddaughter in danger. I wish we lived in a world where good people could get revenge on bad people, but in my experience, revenge just turns good people into bad people."

"That's been my experience too," Faith agreed.

"Did you tell anyone about the missing dog? Anyone close to you?"

"No. It's just me and Jeanie. My wife died ten years ago, and my daughter and her husband died six years ago. My daughter covered Jeanie with her body. That's how Jeanie survived the car crash." He stared ahead. "God, I would give anything to be able to do the same for her now. If I could just sacrifice my own life and bring Fluffy back, I'd do it in a heartbeat."

Faith leaned forward and placed a hand on Donald's shoulder. "She loves her grandfather too, Donald, and she's going to need you now. Please don't blame yourself for what happened."

Donald turned pained eyes up to Faith. "I wish that knowing that made me feel better," he said, "but it doesn't."

CHAPTER SEVENTEEN

The Wolfman had to hand it to Atlanta PD. They were in so far over their head they probably couldn't see the light anymore, but they fought their tails off to protect innocent people.

And innocent dogs. He was overjoyed to hear that the dog fighting ring had been broken up and most of the principles arrested or fled.

It certainly would make his job easier.

He walked around the boarded-up room that at one time had been his K9 training school. For the longest time, he had been the go-to trainer for Atlanta PD. He had trained over two hundred dogs and trained them well. He loved them. He loved taking them from puppies and sending them off as solid professionals—every bit as useful and courageous as their human handlers.

Then that damned ring…

He heard a scuffling noise coming from the back of the building. He walked back to find a stray poking around, probably attracted by the smell of the dog food he still kept here.

"Hey, buddy," he said softly.

The dog leapt back and growled at him, baring its teeth and flattening its ears to its skull. The Wolfman smiled and approached slowly and calmly, keeping his shoulders square and his posture tall.

"Don't worry," he said, "I won't hurt you."

The dog looked left and right, trying to determine the best route of escape. It snarled and snapped to show the Wolfman how dangerous it was and that he had better not pick a fight or the dog would hurt him. The Wolfman kept his calm as he approached the closet near where the dog stood. The dog lunged at him, but he could tell by its cringing posture and the way its tail hung tucked under its legs that the attack was a feint. He kept coming, keeping his eyes on the dog as he opened the door.

The poor creature was emaciated. Its ribs stuck out prominently on its chest, and when the Wolfman opened the closet, the dog's eyes immediately turned to the bags of food. He whined, forgetting for a moment the threat of the large man and thinking only of a chance to soothe its constant hunger.

The Wolfman took a bag and walked to the dishes that lined the wall. The dog's attitude changed immediately. It stopped snapping and approached, cautiously but not fearfully. The Wolfman was happy to see that. The dog had endured much mistreatment at the hands of people, but it was not a stranger to kindness either. There were still some good people in the world.

He poured a good amount of the kibble in the bowl and backed away. The dog looked warily at him, and he smiled again and said, "Go ahead. You can eat."

The dog trotted to the bowl and began to eat, slowly at first, then voraciously, as the chance of a full belly outweighed the fear that this large stranger might hurt him. The Wolfman watched the dog eat and wondered how it could be that anyone would find hurting these creatures more fulfilling than helping them.

His smile faded as he thought of the job he still had to finish. The police had taken care of most of his targets, but there was one who escaped. Francisco Jimenez, real name Gaucho. He was one of the pit bosses. The Wolfman had learned that Gaucho had killed some of the dogs on his way out of the warehouse. Why, he didn't know. For heaven's sake, he could have just left them in the cages. What were they gonna do, rat him out?

But no, he had killed them. Now he would pay. Just like they all had.

The dog finished its meal and cast wondering, grateful eyes on the Wolfman. He started toward the back door, then hesitated and looked back.

The Wolfman would love to have another dog. This one would stay if he commanded it to stay, he knew. He had shown it kindness, and that was enough to earn its lifelong loyalty if he wanted.

But not yet. He still had to avenge Lucy. Then he could find another dog. Maybe this one would return. Probably it would. Dogs remembered kindness. Maybe when his work was done, he could take this one and leave with him. He could travel somewhere out west and find a quiet place in a quiet forest somewhere where the two of them could enjoy the quiet and peaceful existence that they both deserved.

But that day wasn't today.

"Go on," he said. "It's okay. I'll see you again."

The dog dipped its head in acknowledgement and gratitude, then bounded out the door. The Wolfman watched until it disappeared down the alley, then donned his mask, shouldered his pack, and took one last look around his business.

He took a deep breath and squared his shoulders.

Then he left to find Gaucho.

CHAPTER EIGHTEEN

With no leads to follow up on and closing on thirty-six hours with no sleep, the three agents returned to the hotel.

Michael, as always, had no trouble finding sleep. It was one of the qualities Faith most admired in him, the ability to shut his mind off when needed, no matter how desperate the situation. Faith wished she could rest like that.

In the Marine Corps, she had been able to sleep at the drop of a hat and wake just as quickly. That was crucial in an environment where action could occur at any moment, and one needed to be prepared for it. She had kept that skill for the first eight years of her FBI career. Then Trammell…

Then Trammell. It seemed like those were the most important words of her life. Then Trammell. She was able to relax, then Trammell. She was happy, then Trammell. She was confident, then Trammell. She was a great friend, then Trammell.

She wondered sometimes if West's appearance on the scene only exacerbated a problem that existed before him. She wondered if he had never shown up if she might have found someone else to fixate on. Trammell had been the turning point of her life. West was merely the avatar of the depression and trauma that now ruled her.

She checked the time. Two o'clock. Desrouleaux would just be returning from lunch. She picked up her phone and dialed.

"Faith," he said, "Didn't expect to hear from you."

"We hit a lull," she said. "We're catching a few hours of sleep before it's back to the grind."

"I feel you there. I wish I could get a lull."

Faith smiled sympathetically even though Desrouleaux wasn't there to see it. "Have you made any progress?" she asked, trying to sound as casual as possible.

"Well, none of your other acquaintances have been murdered," he said, "No sign of West yet, though. I'm not sure if that means he's made his point and is laying low or if it means the surveillance is working at deterring him."

"So no news?"

“No news, and I hope that means good news, but after two years plus chasing this guy, I don’t know if I should let myself hope that much.”

“Hope springs eternal,” Faith said, “but it never catches you on the way down.”

“A springboard, not a trampoline,” he agreed. “What about you? How are things on your end?”

“Frustrating as usual,” Faith said. “A whole lot of pieces but no idea what the puzzle is yet or how to put it together.”

“Yeah, that doesn’t surprise me. The Syndicate is a serious outfit. I’m surprised the Bureau didn’t want Organized Crime handling this.”

“Well, between you and me, I think the Boss is just trying to fill my time so I don’t go after West again.”

“Yeah, that sounds about right,” he said, “He only does this because he cares about you, you know.”

Faith bristled but controlled her reaction. “Yeah, I know. I just don’t like living looking over my shoulder.”

“Yeah,” he said, “I get that. Well, I gotta get back now. Chavez is staring at me the way my wife stares at me.”

Faith chuckled. "Hopefully, not *exactly* the way your wife stares at you.”

“Oh, Faith,” Desrouleaux said with an exaggerated sigh. “It’s kind of you to think that, but even my wife hasn’t stared at me like that in over a decade.”

Faith laughed and exchanged goodbyes with Desrouleaux. After she hung up, she steepled her fingers together and leaned her elbows forward on the table.

So West had chosen a random person from her past and killed him, then disappeared. Maybe he just wanted Faith to remember he was there.

A memory returned to her of one of the early sessions with West when they were exploring their military service. She recalled it first during the interview with Desrouleaux, but it came back now in sharp and clear detail.

“Well, this Decker was *important to you, Faith, even if you don’t realize it,” West insisted. “You were intimate with him, and even if it seemed to you like it was only scratching an itch, it was certainly far more than that. You chose to reach out for human contact, and when you did, you chose Decker.”*

"I chose him because he had a nice smile and abs," Faith replied, "he's not exactly the one that got away."

"Who is the one that got away?"

Faith thought immediately of Michael, his boyish smile, the laugh he reserved only for those rare occasions when they weren't wracking their brains to try to find some crazed killer or another, the way his face looked when he slept, completely relaxed, free of the years of accumulated stress that eventually overwhelmed even the most resilient of agents.

But that was absurd. She had been in love with Michael, it was true, but it was only a brief infatuation, a puppy love that faded almost as soon as it started.

"I don't really have one," she said.

"Of course you do," West insisted, "but I won't make you tell me who if you wish to keep that thought to yourself. Instead, I'll tell you why Decker was important, why, I suspect, this one that got away was also important."

"Okay," Faith said with a wry smile. "Be my guest."

"You, Faith Bold, are lonely. That is your defining characteristic."

Faith felt herself recoil slightly. She had to fight to keep her voice lighthearted when she said, "Aren't you supposed to try to make me feel better?"

"I'm supposed to help you see things as they truly are," West said, "I'm afraid that more often than not, that involves feeling worse before one feels better. But it is absolutely necessary if you are to gain control of the emotions that now control you."

"My emotions don't control me," Faith said.

"Oh yes, they do," Dr. West replied, "they control everyone. And the emotion that controls you is loneliness. I propose to you, Faith, that you chose Sergeant Decker not because he was the most handsome of the men available. In fact, I would hazard a guess that, in most cases, you would consider a man like Decker one of the least appealing options. But he liked you. He wanted you. Perhaps, in a small way, he even loved you a little. And you wanted that. For just a moment, you wanted to feel like the kind of person who could be loved. That's why you chose him."

"Doesn't everyone want to be loved?" Faith asked.

"They do," West replied, "but we're not talking about everyone. We're talking about you. You and your almost compulsive tendency to

destroy every relationship you have before it can become meaningful enough to hurt you."

Faith's smile faded. "You're becoming pretty meaningful right now, Doctor," she said, putting a warning in her voice.

"Think about it, Faith. Decker liked you. He fulfilled you emotionally, however briefly. Then you left the Marine Corps and never saw him again. What's more, you avoided scenarios where you could potentially see him."

Faith's brow furrowed. "How do you know that?"

"It was in your file. Your unit tracks attendees at all of its reunion events. I believe this is to curtail instances of stolen valor. Either way, you did not attend either reunion."

Faith was speechless. She knew you could track where people were. It never occurred to her that you could track where someone wasn't.

West took advantage of her silence and continued. "You dated your partner, Agent Michael Prince, for roughly thirteen months. Then, when you learned that he was going to invite you to move in with him, you ended things abruptly."

"I... that wasn't... I did... it was a mutual breakup."

"Was it?" West asked, "I'm not so sure."

Faith frowned. "Look, Michael's fine. Michael even told me he doesn't want us to get back together. He's with Ellie now, and he's happy. And I'm happy for him."

"I believe you, Faith. I think, in fact, that whatever jealousy you may feel—"

"I'm not *jealous."*

"—you are also relieved, because now Michael can be your friend and partner. And only *that. The status quo remains the same. And I think you keep Michael closer because it hurts you more to have him close. He is living confirmation of your belief that you're not good enough, and I think that belief, that deep-down* certainty *that you are not enough, is what gets you out of bed in the morning. It's also what will kill you."*

Faith stared ahead as the memory receded. She wasn't sure why she remembered it now. It wasn't directly related to the case or even to the West case aside from the fact that it was a memory of West. Why would she be recalling it now?

She fished for an answer but couldn't find one. Next to her, Turk stirred softly in his sleep.

She looked down at him and felt a powerful surge of love. She smiled. If Faith could be said to have any man in her life she loved above all others, it was this four-legged, furry man with the kindest eyes Faith had ever seen and the personality of a dog a fourth his age.

And she had almost lost him. The second time she had gone after West, he had taken Turk from her, and for two months, Faith was certain that she would never see him again. She would never forget the hopelessness she felt when Turk was gone. She would never forget the joy she felt when he returned.

She thought of the dog fighters, the cruel men who saw these animals as nothing more than disposable violent entertainment. If any of them had hurt her dog, she would…

She would kill them.

It all clicked in Faith's head then. Vincent Mariano had been trying to steal a bait dog. Harvey Harris ran a dogfighting ring. Robert Evans had stolen fighting dogs for Roman Kerry.

All three of their victims had stolen dogs and sent them to die. The killer wasn't hunting the gang. He was hunting the people who murdered dogs. Not just any dogs. Innocent dogs. The dogs of innocent people. Rather than breed their own dogs for fighting, Harris and the others stole dogs from other people and sent them into the pit to die.

If someone had taken Turk, and Turk had died in some dogfighting ring, Faith wasn't certain she could have held back if given the opportunity for revenge. Donald Peterson and Aloysius Farmer had both said they didn't feel sorry for the victims. Even Michael had said that he had never been so angry at a criminal as he was at the dogfighters.

Someone had gone all the way. Someone had killed for revenge. Someone had learned that the gang was killing dogs and had sought retribution.

No, someone had lost their dog to the gang and enacted a very personal retribution.

But who? There had been over twenty dogs in the pits when Michael went undercover. Which of those dogs had an owner with the means and the willingness to kill?

Michael stirred and sat up. "Wow," he said, "I'm getting too old for this. How long did I sleep?"

"Michael, I know who the murderer is," Faith told him.

The rest of Michael's fatigue vanished. He sat upright and stared at her. "Who?"

“I don’t have a name,” she said, “but I have a profile. Our killer is seeking revenge on people who stole dogs that died in the ring.”

“But not the dogs who survived,” Michael said.

“Not yet, anyway,” Faith agreed. “We need the owners of the dogs who died. We need to know where those dogs came from.”

Michael thought a moment, then sighed. “What about Harris, though? Harris never stole a dog himself. Our killer has prioritized people who actually stole the dogs, not the pit bosses or the dog fighters. So whose dog did Harris steal?”

“I don’t know the answer to that question,” Faith admitted, “but I have an idea who might.”

CHAPTER NINETEEN

Garvey was not happy when the agents arrived. "Hey," she said, arms crossed, face set in a scowl. "Which one of you told Roman Kerry that he was going to be released if he cooperated with you?"

Faith blinked. "Neither of us. We never said he was going to be released, just that we would help reduce the charges."

"Why the hell would you tell him that?" Garvey shouted.

"We needed to find the murderer," Faith explained, "and I have a profile. If we can just—"

"You can't just upend the most important case in this department's recent history because it happens to be convenient for your case," Garvey interrupted. "Roman is *my* collar, agents. *Not* yours. Just because you slapped the cuffs on his wrist doesn't suddenly give you the right to decide how his case will be handled."

Faith was stunned by this sudden reversal of attitude in a woman who, up until now, had been solidly on their side. "Detective Garvey, people are dying. We needed the killer."

"Gangsters are dying, agent," Garvey retorted. "And before you get all high and mighty and insist that gangsters are people too, let me remind you that I've spent fifteen years with this department watching those same gangsters orchestrate the deaths of dozens of other people, not to mention trafficking others and hooking thousands more on heroin and cocaine. I'm sorry if it pisses you off to know that their deaths pale in comparison to the deaths of thousands of innocents, but it does, and I'm not about to let one of their leaders shrug off ninety percent of his sentence just because he helps you find a vigilante who's done more to stop this gang than the FBI ever has."

Michael's eyes narrowed. "If I didn't know any better, I'd say you were supporting this killer."

"Yeah, you don't know shit," Garvey spat back. "I want this vigilante off the streets as much as anyone, but I'm not making deals with the devil to stop an imp."

Faith was as upset as Michael was at the animosity from Garvey, but she didn't have time to argue about it now. "We can talk about this later," she said, "we need to speak to Kerry again."

“Of course you do. And that’s all that matters, right?”

Faith had had enough. “Yes, detective,” she said coldly. “It *is* all that matters. You can be as pissy about it as you want, but yes, what matters right now is that we find a serial killer who is currently active in your city. So you can help us, you can get out of our way, or we can have our boss call your boss and get you out of our way.”

Garvey nodded contemptuously. “So that’s it, huh? Nice to finally meet you, agent.”

"You too, detective," Faith spat back. "Now, where's *our* person of interest.”

“Same place you left him,” Garvey replied, “where he’s probably still whining about the fact I haven’t provided a luxury taxi service back to one of the Syndicates whorehouses.”

“Thank you,” Faith said, brushing past her.

As promised, Roman Kerry was right where they left him in the holding cell. As promised, he was indeed whining about the fact that he was still in jail. When he saw the agents, he jammed a finger into their faces and said, “Hey. You two said you’d get me out.”

“No,” Faith said, “we said that we’d help reduce the sentence and the charges. You’re still a gangster with multiple felonies to your name who threatened a federal agent and ran an illegal dogfighting ring.”

“Harris ran that ring. I just stepped in after he died.”

"Which will help reduce, but not eliminate, your sentence. Now, speaking of Harris, I have some questions about him."

“Fuck you. I’m done talking to you. You want info? Get me out of this cage.”

"How ironic," Michael said contemptuously. "The dog wants out of his cage. Maybe we should put you in a ring with another dog and see how it ends up walking away."

“You name the time and place, Mike,” Roman retorted. “I’ll be happy to rip your throat out.”

“Hey,” Faith called, snapping her fingers for attention. “We told you that we’d help reduce the charges if you gave us information leading to your killer. Well, your information led us to a dead end. Give us info that leads to the killer, and those fifteen years turn to two.”

“Yeah, I don’t think so,” Roman said, “See, I made a mistake last time. I forgot that you guys can lie to people just like I can. I trusted you, which was stupid. We’re going back to street rules now. Tit for tat. You scratch my back, I scratch yours. Get me out of here, and I’ll tell you anything you want to know. Until that happens, you can chase your damned tails."

"So fifteen years sounds better than two, huh?" Faith asked.

"I don't believe for a minute that you're going to help me," Roman said, "not unless I force you. So, I'm forcing you. I want a signed statement that I will be cleared of all charges for assisting the FBI in this murder case."

"People in Hell want ice water," Michael retorted.

"And people on the other side of the cage want answers," Roman retorted. "No one's getting what they want until I get mine."

Faith could see in the set of Roman's jaw that he meant it. They had exhausted his usefulness. She sighed and said, "Well, maybe prison won't be so bad. You seem like a sweet guy. I'm sure you'll make friends."

"Yeah?" Roman sneered. "You want to be my friend, agent? Bet you'd look real nice with your face down and your ass up."

"All right," Michael said, "Enjoy prison."

The three agents left the room. Garvey met them outside, her arms crossed. "Get what you need?" she asked sarcastically.

"Detective Garvey," Faith said stiffly. "I fully understand that you're upset right now. I'm pretty sure you and I are upset for similar reasons. So we can butt heads, or you can deal with the fact that the FBI is in charge right now. Make our jobs easier, and we make yours easier."

"By giving my suspects a get out of jail free card?"

"By taking a murderer off the streets," Faith replied, "in addition to orchestrating a raid that by your own admission is the biggest bust you've seen in your career. In addition to busting the three primary revenue streams of the Georgia Syndicate in Atlanta. You're choosing to be angry over a relatively minor detail and ignoring the great help we've done your city, your department and your career. And that's fine. I truly don't care how you feel about this. But you *will* put yourself and your department at our disposal, or I *will* go over your head and make sure that whoever I have to talk to knows exactly why. I don't have time to play nice anymore."

Garvey glared at her, and Faith was certain that if Garvey could have teleported her back to Philadelphia, she would have. After a moment, though, the glare faded, and Garvey nodded. "Fair enough. You have your job, I have mine. Up until now, our interests have coincided, and, like you said, you helped us out. Okay. I won't promise to support you if you try to reduce Roman's sentence, but I'll help you find your killer."

"Well, you'll be happy to know that Roman has declined to be of assistance," Michael said, "so feel free to throw the book at him."

Garvey lifted an eyebrow. "So he got stupid again, huh? Can't say I'm surprised."

"Listen," Faith said, "the killer is someone who lost a dog, probably recently. Someone who's intentionally targeting people who stole dogs that ended up dead in the pits."

"So what about Harris then? He wasn't stealing dogs."

"Exactly. He's the outlier, and he's the one this case hinges on. We've been operating under the assumption that it was personal with Mariano, and that the killer was escalating with Evans, but I think we have it backwards. I think the killer went to the one who mattered most first. I think that's why there was a struggle. He needed Harris coherent when he saw him. He needed Harris to know who he was and why he was doing this. He needed to hear Harris admit to his crimes. That gave Harris a chance to escape, which is why there were signs of a struggle in his case but not in anyone else's case."

"So you wanted Roman to tell you if any of Harris's dogs had been killed lately," Garvey surmised, "so you could track those dogs back to their owners."

"Exactly," Faith said, "but he's not talking, so we need to talk to the other gangsters present at the pits."

"All right," Garvey said, "I can help with that. I can't make anyone talk, though. Even the underlings are clamming up."

"We have to try," Faith said.

Try they did. They spent the next two hours interviewing prisoners and getting nothing. The prisoners, interestingly enough, were more than willing to divulge details of their own involvement in the ring. A few were pit bosses. A few were trainers. A few were handlers and a few were what they called "ticket-takers," people who took spectator fees and bets and handled the flow of cash. Two of them were security. They happily detailed their violent defense of the gang's right to make innocent dogs murder each other, but when it came to talking about Harris and which of his dogs hadn't fared well in the pit, they clammed up.

"For God's sake," Faith said in exasperation after the tenth interview once more yielded nothing. "Harris is dead. What's he going to do to you?"

“It ain’t about that,” the man said, “It’s about honor. We don’t snitch on each other.”

Faith pressed her fingers to the bridge of her nose. “Honor? Seriously? You guys stole pets and trained them to eat each other. What kind of honor is that?”

The man drew himself up with sickening pride. “We’re wolves, agent. Sure, we eat sheep. But we don’t eat other wolves.”

“Charming,” Faith said, rolling her eyes. “I’m sure you’ll find that to be exactly the same when you share a room with a lifer. Good luck with that.”

The police officers filed him away, his chest still absurdly puffed out. Faith turned to Michael, hands on her hips and said, “So what do we do now?”

“I don’t know,” Michael said, shaking his head. Then his eyes widened. “Actually, I do.”

He left the interrogation room suddenly. Faith and Turk followed on his heels. He found Garvey and said, “The others arrested that night, the ones who weren’t affiliated with the gang. Where did they go?”

Garvey lifted an eyebrow. “They’re at county waiting for their arraignment. Why? You think they know something?”

“I don’t know, but if they do, I think they might be willing to talk,” Michael said. “The gangsters all have the snitches get stitches motto drilled into their brains. We won’t get anything from them.”

"All right," Garvey said. "You want to go to county, or do you want me to send someone here?"

“What’s faster?”

“I’ll have them bring someone here. Then they only need to proccss him instead of him and you.”

“Have them send all of them here,” Faith said. “We’ll talk until we get an answer.”

***

Benjamin Ritter was very clearly not the same kind of person as the gangsters Faith and Michael had been talking to before now. He practically shook with fear, and when he accepted the water Faith brought him, he spilled some, bringing it to his lips.

“Jail’s not so fun a place to be, is it?” Michael said sympathetically.

Benjamin swallowed and shook his head.

“People being mean to you, Ben?” Michael asked.

“Or are they being too nice?’ Faith said.

Ben shivered. "N—no one's hurt me yet, but… look, agents, I know I made a mistake, okay? I shouldn't have been in that place. It's not for me."

“Really?” Faith asked, “because you told Detective Garvey that was your ninth visit to the pits. If it wasn’t for you, why did you go back?”

Ben swallowed. “I… I know I shouldn’t have—”

“We’ve established that, Ben,” Michael said. “Read you loud and clear. You did wrong. Believe me, we have no confusion on that point. The reason we’re here now is because you have a chance to do right.”

Ben blinked. “I… I don’t understand.”

“That’s okay,” Michael said, his voice laced with contempt. “I wouldn’t expect you to. So let me help you out. We believe we know who’s been electrocuting people to death with a shock collar. You heard about that, right?”

Ben nodded. “Some of the guys at the warehouse were talking about it.”

“Look at you, keeping your ears open,” Faith said. “That’s good. That’s real good.”

“It sure is,” Michael said, “it means you might actually be able to do good.”

A lightbulb went off in Ben’s head. He finally realized that if he cooperated with the agents, then they would be inclined to release him. “Y-Yeah. Okay. What do you want to know?”

“Are you familiar with Harvey Harris?” Michael asked.

“H-Bomb? Yeah, he was the master of ceremonies. The dogfights were his baby. He was the one who first organized them. He built the league and everything, created the brackets, wrote the rules. He was turning it into a legitimate sport that…”

He saw the stony faces of the agents and Turk’s narrowed eyes and decided that it probably wasn’t in his best interests to speak so glowingly of dogfighting. He swallowed and finished with, “Anyway, yeah. I know him.”

“Wonderful,” Faith said, “How many of his own dogs fought?”

“Well, he didn’t fight his own dogs much anymore. He’d find dogs for other people, but the only dog I know that he fought under his own name was a German shepherd he called Huntress.”

Faith tried to keep the excitement from showing on her face. “What happened to Huntress?”

Ben shrugged. “Well… she wasn’t a very good huntress.”

“Lost her fight, huh?” Michael asked.

"Badly. She didn't even fight back. She just stood there and let herself get literally eaten." He shook his head. "I couldn't believe it. A lot of people were pissed. Harris talked her up, you know? She told everyone she was small but fierce. Talked about how he had seen her take down powerlifters and bodybuilders five times her size. Said she scared the hell out of all the other dogs in the pits. Then she didn't fight. Didn't even try to protect herself, not even when the other dog bit out her—"

“All right,” Michael interrupted. “We get the point.”

“Now this is the important part, Ben,” Faith said, uncrossing her arms and leaning forward on the table. “Do you know who Huntress’s owner was before Harris stole her?”

Ben shook his head. “They never told us any of that. I didn’t even know that he stole the dog. I thought they raised them from puppies to be fighters.”

Michael sighed. “See, that’s a problem, Ben. That helps us, but only a little. Meaning we can only help you a little. I don’t know if you’re aware, but betting on dogfights nine times in a row carries a sentence of up to three years each. That’s twenty-seven years, Ben. That’s a lot of life. You’re what, twenty-seven, twenty-eight?”

“Twenty-nine,” Ben said.

“Twenty-nine. So you’d be… fifty-six when you get out?” Michael whistled. “That’s a long time. Well, with the info you gave us, maybe we can shave a third of that off. That means you get out at forty-seven. I guess that’s not too bad—”

“Wait!” Ben said, “Wait! I… I can tell you what she looked like. She… she had a little divot in her ear, right out of the top. Right he—” he reached for Turk’s ear, and Turk growled low in his throat. Ben jerked his hand back and said, “Um… right on the top. She also had light brown fur, lighter than his, almost tan. Uh, and blue eyes. I guess she was a husky mix or something.”

Michael smiled. “Now that’s more like it, Ben. All right. We’ll see what we can do about these charges.”

“Oh, thank you!” Ben cried. “Thank you so much! I’m so sorry. I’ll never do anything like that ever again, I swear!”

“Uh huh,” Michael said.

He nodded at the officer, who led the still profusely grateful Ben out the door. He turned to Faith and said, "You want to talk to the others, or do you want to start looking for this dog?"

"We start looking for the dog," Faith said. "If we find this dog, then we find the killer."

"You're sure of that?"

Faith looked at Turk next to her and thought of everything she would do to anyone who hurt him, everything she wanted to do to West just for threatening to take him from her. She had been fortunate enough to get Turk back. Huntress's original owner hadn't. He had no reason left to control himself.

"Yes," she said, "I'm sure."

CHAPTER TWENTY

They went to Garvey's office and looked up dogs that matched that description in the city's registry. Dogs were, apparently, quite popular in Atlanta. There were nine hundred thirty-two shepherd/husky mixes in the city, and the number skyrocketed if you extended the search to a fifty-mile radius. This would take some time to dig through.

"Screw that," Garvey said, "I'll get us some help."

Soon, a dozen officers were helping the three of them look through the city's records. Faith divided up the list evenly, with each of the searchers looking through sixty-two different dogs. That definitely saved time, but it still took them over an hour to get through the list.

More concerningly, they didn't find an answer. Of the nine hundred thirty-two dogs, five hundred twenty-seven were crossed off immediately as not matching the description closely enough. Ben was particular about the color of the fur, and most of the animals he listed had dark fur since both huskies and shepherds tended toward dark fur.

Of the ones that remained, three hundred eighty-one had died months or years ago and had yet to be removed from the county's list. That left only twenty-four dogs that could potentially have been the one Harris called Huntress, but the owners of each of those dogs were able to confirm that their dogs were alive and well and had never so much as run away from home, let alone been stolen.

They were at another dead end.

Faith, Michael and Garvey reconvened in Garvey's office after the search. All three of them wore their frustration on their faces.

"It could be that the dog wasn't registered," Garvey said reluctantly. "The county estimates that only twenty-three percent of pets are registered. The rest are just… out there."

Faith's lips thinned. Her arms were crossed over her chest, hugging her shoulders tightly. "So there could be another two thousand dogs out there that meet that description and there's no way to find them."

"We could check online again," Michael said. "See if any dogs matching that description have been reported missing like Fluffy Face was."

He didn't sound very hopeful, though, and Faith shared his lack of confidence. "That's a crap shoot. We got lucky with Fluffy Face. We might not get so lucky with Huntress."

"Well, what else can we do?" Michael asked.

Faith sighed irritably. He had a point. She looked out the window at the sun, which was now halfway below the horizon. Another day was approaching its end, and they still didn't have a suspect. "All right," she said reluctantly. "Let's get people looking through social media."

"Wait," Garvey said, her eyes widening. "The K9 records!"

Faith and Michael turned to look at her, and she explained, "The police and sheriff's department registers their K9s under a different database than the civilian registry. If the dog stolen was a K9 or a former K9, then we might be able to find it there."

Faith felt a renewed flash of hope. "All right," she said, "let's look there."

Garvey opened the website, and they began to scan through the database. There were two hundred thirty-eight K9s between the police and sheriff's department and another eighty-four operated by the FBI and the DEA in the greater Atlanta metropolitan area. Quite a few, but less than the civilian registries.

Even better, the registry for each dog listed their status, so the agents were able to quickly dismiss any dogs listed as active duty. Of the ones that were left, a few phone calls confirmed that the ones listed as retired were still alive and well and enjoying some time with their new owners.

That left twenty-six dogs listed as deceased or unknown. Of those dogs, only one matched the description of light brown fur, so light it was almost tan.

Faith, Michael and Garvey stared at the image of Lucy, a nine-year-old Shepherd/Husky mix who up until six months ago was a distinguished member of the PDs K9 division. She had retired once she reached the mandatory retirement age of nine and was listed as sold to a man named Eric Ciccolo, a K9 trainer who had trained Lucy and many other dogs for the police department. He had developed an attachment to Lucy and was allowed to buy her when she retired.

Two months ago, Lucy had been reported as missing by Ciccolo. No note existed to say what came of that investigation, if there was one.

Lucy definitely tended more toward German Shepherd than to Husky. She had the shape and build of a shepherd, along with the coarse short hair. The only visible sign of her mixed heritage was her beautiful sky-blue eyes.

And her fur, as Ben had reported, was a very light brown, so light it was almost tan. The tan was a similar pattern as Turk's chestnut and chocolate, but much lighter. In some places, it was so light it nearly blended into the white of her paws and underbelly.

She was a beautiful dog. Turk whined mournfully as he looked at the picture.

Faith ruffled his fur as she looked up Eric Ciccolo. The smiling image of a bearded man in his early forties with a barrel chest and a muscular figure came up. Ciccolo had spent fifteen years as the owner of CK9 Dog Training School, an academy specifically tailored to training police and government K9 dogs. The CK9 website proudly announced that Ciccolo had trained over two hundred dogs and that all of his dogs had gone on to have distinguished careers with their respective organizations and had incurred no disciplinary notes.

This guy was good. He couldn't be as good at that job as he was unless he truly cared about his dogs. And Faith knew how far someone would go to protect dogs they cared about.

Or to avenge them.

"Damn," Garvey said, "that's her. That's Huntress."

"Lucy," Faith corrected. "Let's not use the name her killer gave her."

Garvey lifted an eyebrow at Faith's rather unnecessary correction, but the look on her face made her think better of whatever retort she planned to give.

"All right," Faith said, "we have our suspect. Garvey, you take some officers and go to Ciccolo's home address. Michael, Turk and I will visit CK9."

"Works for me," Garvey replied. "Are you two armed?"

"We are," Faith confirmed, "but I hope to God we won't have to use our weapons."

***

CK9, not surprisingly, was closed. Permanently. Boards shuttered the windows, and a simple paper sign hung on the door informing prospective customers bluntly that CK9 had permanently ceased operations. The paper was tattered, and the words faded, but still legible. The date listed was for fifty-seven days ago, shortly after Lucy was taken and then killed. Eric Ciccolo had found another avenue of employment.

Faith knelt down and jimmied the lock, a skill she had used a few times before on a case. Once the three of them were inside, they looked for any sign of Ciccolo.

There was some dust, but far less than there should have been. Even more telling was the computer plugged into the desk, still running. Ciccolo might have closed his business, but he still used the property.

For what, though?

Turk put his nose to the ground, sniffing for clues. Michael and Faith walked through the emptied offices and training rooms, noting the posters of Eric with different dogs and talking with different officers.

"This guy really loved his dogs," Michael said, pointing at a poster of Eric, bursting with pride and grinning from ear to ear, handing a dog its certificate ribbon. The dog itself—not Lucy, but another Shepherd—looked at Eric with a love bordering on devotion, and Faith felt a twinge as she recalled her fear when Turk was taken from her.

They walked back to the kennels, and there they finally found the disrepair they expected to find in the entire building. The room was caked with dust, so thick that Turk's paws left visible tracks as he moved ahead of them. He whined softly and mournfully as he walked through the empty cages, their hinges rusted and, in some cases, destroyed, the doors hanging lopsidedly. The room smelled stale and musty, and Faith suspected the three of them were the first living things to enter in some time.

Ciccolo had avoided this place. He had been so distraught by Lucy's death that he had shut down his business and avoided reminding himself of her. At least as much as possible.

But he had kept the building. There must be a reason.

Faith's phone buzzed. Garvey.

"Hey, he's not here," Garvey said. "I can't break in without a warrant, and that will take at least the rest of the day. Should I get one?"

No sooner had he asked that than Turk started barking excitedly. "Hold that thought," Faith said.

She hung up and followed the sound of Turk's cries. They led her and Michael to a small room adjacent to the kennels. Once inside, Faith knew for sure that they were on the right trail.

The room appeared to be a small storage closet used for training supplies. There were leashes, collars and a few bodysuits that handlers would wear for dogs to practice bringing suspects down. There were other miscellaneous supplies—food and water bowls, vests, et cetera—but the objects that attracted Turk's attention were none of those things.

The particular collars Turk was barking at were stacked in the middle of the room. There were seventeen in all.

Each band had an electrode attached to it. The electrodes seemed to be from different sources that Faith couldn't identify. Some were bulky things with wires sticking out everywhere and loops of magnets and carbon brushes visible inside. Others were far slimmer and seemed like little more than standard electric collar shock units.

Next to the collars was a pile of remotes. There were a few modified tv remotes and a few video game controllers. One was a large RC controller for RC cars.

This was Ciccolo's armory.

Faith's phone buzzed again. Garvey sounded testy when Faith answered.

"Hey, do me a favor. Don't tell me to hold on, then hang up on me and not call back. That makes me think you're in danger, and I should call units to come to your location."

"You should call one unit to come to my location," Faith said, "to pick up the evidence I just found. You should also tell all of the units currently out in the field to be on the lookout for Eric Ciccolo."

Garvey paused a split second. "What did you find?"

Faith looked at the pile of collars and remotes. "Murder weapons."

CHAPTER TWENTY ONE

Eric parked across the street from the small, dirty bungalow set in the hillside overlooking the western portion of Atlanta. At one point, this bungalow had been the office of a firing range. The range was still used occasionally by amateur shooters and hunters, but the office had long since closed.

At the moment, the bungalow was the hideout for one Francisco Jimenez, known to his fellow low-lifes as Gaucho. He had been here since the raid on the warehouse a few days ago and was probably trying to figure out how he was going to stay away from some no doubt very angry employers who were running out of available targets for their frustration.

In a way, it would be poetic justice if Gaucho were killed by the very employers who paid him to kill, but Eric didn't want that for him. He wanted to be the one to watch Gaucho die. He was the last of the dog-murderers who needed to be brought to justice.

Well, that wasn't exactly true. The entire Georgia Syndicate needed to fall, but Eric knew his limits. He was one man, and while he had a skill set that allowed him to make the small difference he had made so far, he was under no illusions that he could somehow destroy an entire crime family.

So, he would take this one last killer out, and then he would work in the shadows, investigating the Syndicate and passing information along to the FBI, the DEA and the ATF to aid them in their fight to bring the organization down. He hadn't worked out all of those details yet, but he would save that until after he took care of his own mission.

This was it. This was the end of this chapter of his life. After today, the Wolfman was gone. He would go back to being Eric Ciccolo, private citizen, until he figured out what identity he wanted to assume when he turned unofficial investigator.

Maybe he wouldn't bother with an identity. The Wolfman had a purpose to it. The last thing the dog killers saw was the image of their own victims. That made sense. Since he would be working clandestinely and in a support factor rather than as someone pulling the trigger himself, it would just be frivolous ego that made him don an identity. If they asked him who he was, he would just say nobody.

Nobody. That name worked as well as any.

"Nobody," he whispered softly.

How he wished that were true. If he were nobody, maybe Lucy would still be alive.

He smiled softly as he recalled the day he first saw Lucy. She was so small and adorable, just a little ball of cream and tan with the most beautiful blue eyes he'd ever seen. He'd joked with his wife at the time that those were the most beautiful eyes he had ever seen, even more beautiful than her own.

Of course, *that* set of beautiful blue eyes had eventually fallen on one of the other partners at her firm, and now the two of them lived somewhere in Colorado helping sufferers of ski accidents sue the winter resorts in Aspen. He didn't miss his ex-wife.

But God, he missed Lucy.

He read somewhere that there were religious texts that commanded men to give the last of their food to their dogs before their wife, to let their families starve to death before they let their hounds starve to death. He had no idea if that was really written anywhere or if the website had just made something up to be shocking and sensational, but he agreed with the sentiment. After all, a dog would never cheat you. A dog would never betray you. A dog would live its entire life devoted to pleasing you.

A dog would die rather than go against its owner's wishes.

A pang of guilt hit Eric at that. The first man he had killed, Harris, told him that Lucy hadn't even fought. She had sat there and allowed herself to get killed rather than fight back. Eric trained all of his dogs to refrain from violence unless commanded to use it, and Lucy had been the best of all of his dogs. He could fully believe that she had sat there, knowing she would die but preferring that to disappointing him.

He hated himself for that. He wished with all of his heart that he had taught her instead to defend herself at all costs. Maybe if he had, she could have survived long enough for him to rescue her.

Well, he couldn't fix the past, but he could change the future. He could, and had, avenged her and all of the other dogs that had been killed by that horrible dog fighting ring.

Except for one man, and that one man would get his comeuppance today. He glanced at the passenger seat where his tools waited. He had brought a handgun today. He was fairly sure that Gaucho was armed, and while he preferred to kill Gaucho the way he killed all of his victims, he wasn't so set on it that he would risk his own death. If Gaucho got the drop on him, he would do what he had to do.

The collar today was a new one. The last one had been rendered unusable after Eric had nearly melted Robert Evans' neck with it. He realized that it was dangerous for him to allow his emotions to take over like that, but there was a sense of triumph watching the body of that killer jerk around, abused just like the body of his victim. The only regret he had was that Jeanie Peterson would never know that Fluffy Face's kidnapper had been punished for his crime. Maybe when she was older, Eric would look her up and leave her a note.

Or not. Children moved on so easily, and Jeanie was young. It was possible that she would be able to push away her guilt and think only of the good times she had with Fluffy Face. Eric would hate to remind her of her dog's brutal end unnecessarily.

No, those memories were for him to carry. That was the burden he chose when he adopted the Wolfman.

Eric looked in the rearview mirror. The snarling face of a wolf, the ancestor of all dogs, looked back at him.

"One more hunt," he said softly, "one more kill."

He looked out the window at the darkening twilight. A perfect ending to a perfect career. He grabbed the handgun and the collar and stepped out of the car.

CHAPTER TWENTY TWO

Garvey stared at the pile of evidence on the floor. In addition to the collars and remotes, they found three different wolf masks. Ciccolo evidently had adopted a persona as the killer. In the office, Michael sat in front of the computer, desperately trying to find any indication of where Ciccolo would go next.

Turk stood next to Faith, who in turn stood next to Garvey. His tail switched back and forth as he stared at the pile of evidence. He looked up at Faith and whined softly.

Faith knew what he was saying. They needed to hurry.

"Damn," Garvey whispered softly. "I never would have suspected him."

"Did you know him?" Faith asked.

"Well, no," Garvey admitted. "What I mean is that I would never have suspected someone connected to law enforcement. If someone was going to go vigilante, I would have expected a civilian."

"Well, technically speaking, Ciccolo is a civilian," Faith pointed out. "He contracts with the police department, but he never swore an oath."

"Not that that's an excuse," Garvey added.

She sounded like she was trying to remind herself of that point. Faith didn't blame her. Considering what she knew of their victims and what she and Michael had seen of the gang and the people involved in it, she had a hard time drumming up any sympathy for the people who had died.

But she had a job to do, and just because the people you targeted were bad people didn't mean you sacrificed your values to do it.

She felt a stab of guilt at that thought. Faith herself had compromised a shocking number of her own values over the course of her pursuit of West. From confronting and accusing people with no evidence other than her own intuition to speaking with witnesses behind the Bureau's back to even assaulting a suspect and breaking down his door, Faith had oftentimes wondered who exactly she was and if she still believed the things she believes.

Well, she had suffered her own consequences, and whatever opinions she might hold, Ciccolo needed to suffer his.

"Did you see any signs of flight at Ciccolo's house?" Faith asked.

"Well, we didn't go inside yet," Garvey replied. "I went ahead and applied for that warrant on the way over here, so we'll probably be able to enter the property tomorrow."

"By that time, he could be halfway to Canada," Faith said.

"He could already be halfway to Canada," Garvey pointed out, "but I think I've seen enough vigilantism for one lifetime. I don't intend to become one myself."

"Fait enough," Faith replied, "but I think we can justify this as probable cause."

"Right," Garvey said. "I'll send some officers back over to enter and see what they can find."

While she radioed instructions, Faith headed to Michael. Michael was digging through Eric's internet searches, trying to see if he could glean any info.

"Anything useful?" Faith asked.

Michael sighed. "Well, he's getting his collars from a website called Protected Pooches. He's using a pseudonym, Vincent Harris."

Faith whistled. "He's using his victims' names as his handle. That's cold."

Michael shrugged. "Can't say I blame him. This is the first case I've worked that I sympathize with the killer more than with his victims."

Faith looked over at Turk, who now rested next to the back door. "I know what you mean," she said. "Have you found a trail for Vincent Harris yet?"

"Nothing yet. The electrical products are mostly coming from hardware parts stores. I do see two orders for a cattle prod, but those are under the name Francis Evans."

"Evans was another victim," Faith reminded him. "That might be something."

"Yeah, but who's Francis?" Michael asked. "None of the gang members were named Francis, unless I'm missing something."

"No," Faith said, "they weren't."

"So is it a completely made-up name or is there someone we don't know out there in Eric's sights?"

Faith's blood chilled as she imagined their killer out there hunting while they were so close to finding him but at the same time so far away. That had happened a lot. In fact, it had happened more often than now. Faith and Michael never worked with the slow and methodical killers. It was always the crazed ones pushing a frenzied pace that fell in their laps.

"I'm not sure," Faith replied, "but I'm leaning toward the latter."

Michael sighed. "Well, there are…" he clicked a few more buttons, then said, "eight thousand two hundred four Francis's in Atlanta. Male Francis's anyway, although there were women at the dogfighting ring, so maybe it's wrong to assume all of his victims will be men."

"That's too many people to dig through anyway," Faith said. "Eric will have killed his next victim by then. If he is looking for a victim."

"You think he might have run already?" Michael asked. "I overheard you and Garvey talking about it."

"I think it's possible," Faith said. "He was targeting members of the dogfighting ring, specifically members he saw as directly responsible for the deaths of the dogs. Since we broke up the ring, there's no one else out there killing dogs. Not in Atlanta anyway. Eric might consider the job done. He probably knows we're here, especially if he was following the dog fighting ring. So he knows we're looking for him. He could have decided not to be findable."

Michael tapped the edge of the desk and shook his head. "I don't think so. We didn't arrest everyone there. We got half the gangsters, but half of them escaped. Not all of them would have been directly involved with the dogs, but it's a good bet that some of them were. And the other organizers are among them. It's true that Eric's prioritizing people who directly caused dogs to die, but I don't think he'll stop there. I think he'll keep going until every member of the gang is wiped out."

"So who's he going after then?" Faith said.

Michael shook his head. "Therein lies the rub." Then his eyes widened. "Wait. I think I figured it out."

"What is it?" Faith asked.

"Francis Evans," Michael said, "the Evans part is obviously Robert Evans, but the Francis part threw me off. There isn't anyone named Francis that we know of in the gang."

"Okay," Faith said, "I'm not following."

"There's no one named Francis," Michael said, "but there is a Francisco."

Faith's eyes widened. "Francisco Jimenez."

"Gaucho," Michael confirmed. "He was the pit boss who arranged the meeting between me and the organizers. That's who Eric is going after next."

"Where is Gaucho?" Faith asked.

"No idea," Michael said.

Garvey returned to the office then. "All right," she said, "I have officers on their way back to Ciccolo's house."

"Good," Faith said, "tell them to look for anything that refers to a Francisco Jimenez or to Gaucho."

Garvey lifted an eyebrow. "You think he's going after Gaucho next?"

"I am almost certain of it," Faith said, "what's more, I'm almost certain that he's going after Gaucho as we speak."

"So how do we find him?" Garvey asked.

"I think I know someone who can help," Faith said.

***

"You guys are crazy if you think I'm going to help you," Roman said, jaw jutting defiantly forward as he faced the four of them.

Turk growled low in his throat, but Roman sat inside the holding cell protected by thick steel bars. He sneered at Turk and said, "I wish we could have seen you fight, little dog. Ceasar would have eaten you for breakfast."

"He's after Gaucho," Faith said.

"Who's after Gaucho?"

"The killer. He's hunting Gaucho right now, intending to kill him. So, we're here to make a new deal: you tell us where we can find Gaucho, and we'll keep our original bargain. We talk to the DA, recommend leniency, and point out how instrumental you were in finding the killer and bringing him to justice. Fifteen years turns to five, out in two on good behavior."

Roman sneered at them. "I thought I told you already, I don't talk unless I walk."

Garvey stepped ahead of Faith. "Let's clarify something, Roman. You don't have power here. The best you can do right now is make it easier for the murderer we're hunting to kill your comrades in arms. We'd rather you didn't, but the fact is we're not going to bend over backwards helping a gang leader serve less time so we can stop someone from killing other gangsters. We're doing you a *favor*,

Roman. We're not begging for help. At best, you represent a chance to solve this case conveniently. We will solve it without you. In fact, we've already solved it. We're just apprehending our suspect. Again, though, we're not going to fight all that hard to convince you to help out your fellow gangsters. We'll just point out to the press that we tried to ask for your help, but you chose to let more of your friends die instead."

Roman glared at Garvey, but his shoulders deflated slightly. “You think you’re so much better than me, don’t you?”

“So much better that I have absolutely no interest in hearing your opinions to the contrary,” Garvey said, “Now you can help us find the man we’re looking for or you can rot in jail until you’re old and gray. It’s all the same to me.”

Roman jutted his jaw out and stared at Garvey. After a moment, Garvey shrugged and said, “All right. Good luck in prison.”

The three agents followed Garvey from the room. Just before Faith closed the door, Roman called, “Wait.”

He sounded defeated, and when Faith turned and saw the dejection on his face, she knew they had won.

CHAPTER TWENTY THREE

“Well,” Michael said, “looks like it’s Roman’s lucky day.”

Faith pulled in behind the pickup truck parked across the street from a worn-down bungalow that backed up to the small mountain range just west of the city. Garvey pulled her cruiser behind them.

It was generous to call it a mountain range. Just a few hills, really, where Garvey informed the agents that hunters would come to practice their aim and fine-tune their weapons.

Garvey ran the license plate and, a moment later, confirmed that the truck was Ciccolo's. "Okay, "she said, "we're in business."

Faith looked up at the bungalow, barely visible in the fading light. “We should hurry,” she said. “I don’t mean to further mess with your protocol, Detective, but this might be an ask questions later scenario.”

As if to punctuate Faith’s point, a scream pierced the night. Instantly the four humans: Faith, Michael, Garvey and a uniform she had brought with her, and Turk sprinted up the path to the bungalow.

As they ran, Faith drew her weapon. She felt bile rise in her throat. For the first time in her career, she hoped she didn’t have to use her weapon on a suspect. Not that she normally enjoyed shooting criminals, but she didn’t usually feel bad about it.

She would feel bad if she had to use it now. Eric wasn’t innocent. She knew that, but it was hard to think of him as guilty either. What had he done except avenge innocent dogs and innocent people by ridding the city of a few lowlifes?

She knew that was a dangerous mindset to have, but the fact remained that a part of Faith hoped they would find Gaucho already dead when they made it inside.

That turned out not to be the case. Turk, of course, reached the building before they did. Faith heard loud barking and another shriek. Then she and the other three sprinted into the bungalow.

Ciccolo was there, wearing his wolf mask and holding a shock collar in his left hand. His right hand held a handgun, but he wasn’t aiming at Turk or the officers. He was aiming it at the cowering, prostrate form of Gaucho. When the agents walked in, he turned his weapon to them, then back to Gaucho. The hesitation allowed the officers to spread out and cover Ciccolo with their own weapons.

Gaucho turned wide eyes toward his rescuers. His eyes widened even further when he saw Michael. Then they narrowed in anger. "*Pinche pendejo!*" he shouted. "Screw you, Mike! This is your fault!"

"You keep telling yourself that," Michael said drily.

"Eric Ciccolo," Garvey said, leveling her weapon at Eric and approaching slowly while the other officer flanked him. "You're under arrest. Put the weapon down and put your hands in the air."

Ciccolo looked at the approaching officers while Turk and Faith flanked the other side and Micheal joined Garvey in the middle. Then he looked back at Gaucho. His fingers tightened around the trigger, and Turk jumped in between the two criminals.

"No!" Faith cried.

But Eric didn't shoot at Turk. Instead, he lifted his handgun and aimed at a point above Garvey and Michael's head. He fired three quick bursts.

Faith looked up just in time to see one of the light fixtures start to fall. "Watch out!" she shouted.

Michael and Garvey looked up and jumped backward at the last possible second. The uniform, shocked by the sudden collapse, took his focus off of Eric, and the big man slammed a meaty fist into his temple. The officer went out cold, his gun clattering across the floor.

Gaucho tried to take advantage of the commotion. He got to his feet and started for the exit, but Michael reached him first, grabbing his shoulders and throwing him to the ground. "Uh uh," he said, "you're under arrest too, buddy."

"You're not my buddy!" Gaucho shouted as he writhed ineffectually underneath Michael's knee.

"You're still under arrest," Michael said, wrenching the criminal's left arm around and clapping handcuffs onto his wrist.

While Michael dealt with Gaucho and Garvey assisted her fallen officer, Faith and Turk rushed after Eric. The big man moved with surprising agility, leaping over a counter and vaulting through an open window.

Faith cursed and sprinted for the front door, knowing she would lose him if she tried the direct route. She needed to get to flat ground and flank him. Turk followed easily, though, and by the time Faith came back to the side of the building, he had cornered Eric.

Eric kept running, and for a terrifying moment, Faith thought he was going to kick Turk. Instead, he leapt over the dog, showing surprising dexterity for a man his size.

Turk hesitated, probably just as shocked as Faith was. That allowed Eric time to leap into a shallow crevice and sprint toward the mountain. Turk leaped after him, and Eric leaped out of the crevice. Turk followed and he jumped into the crevice again, keeping Turk occupied so the dog couldn't catch up to him.

Faith sprinted on the outside of the crevice and shouted ahead to Turk. “Stay inside!”

Turk looked back, confused by the command, and Eric dove behind a boulder. Faith skidded to a halt, knowing that Eric would be waiting for her behind the rock, gun drawn.

Turk didn’t stop. He barked and ran toward the boulder, believing he had his prey quarried.

“Turk!” Faith shouted. “Stop!”

Turk did stop. Right behind the boulder. He snarled and snapped, but backed away as he did so, watching Eric warily.

Faith couldn’t see behind the rock, but she knew Turk was watching Eric’s weapon. She sprinted forward, no longer caring for her own safety. “Eric, don’t you dare hurt my dog!”

She skidded to a stop behind the boulder and saw Eric pointing his weapon at Turk. His face wrestled with his decision, and Faith could see his hands shake slightly as he aimed the handgun at her dog.

Faith leveled her handgun at Eric and slowly circled until she was in his field of vision. “Be smart about this, Eric. There’s four of us and one of you, and we have a dog. I know you’re not a bad man. I know you aren’t going to hurt innocent people who are just doing their jobs. Francisco Jimenez is being placed under arrest and will be charged with animal cruelty.”

Eric looked at her then back at Turk. His hand tightened around his weapon.

Faith kept her hands steady and said, “I know you won’t hurt my dog either, Eric. That’s not you.”

Eric looked back at Faith, then at Turk. Then he relaxed slightly. “You’re right, agent,” he called. “I won’t. I’m going to lower my weapon now. I’m done.”

Faith kept her handgun trained on Eric until the big man lowered his handgun then backed away, his hands in the air. Normally, she would keep a weapon on the suspect until he was handcuffed, but she knew that wasn't necessary this time. She holstered her weapon and walked to Eric.

Eric was compliant, as she knew he would be. He allowed her to cuff him, and she was grateful that his compliance allowed her to be gentle.

"Would you mind removing my mask?" he asked. "It's hot as blazes out here, and since you know who I am, there's no point in wearing it anymore."

"Sure," Faith said.

She carefully removed the mask, and Eric sighed with relief. "Thank you, agent," he said. He looked down at Turk, who had also calmed considerably now that the suspect was apprehended. "You have a good dog there," he said, "very well-trained. A lot of K9s would have attacked me in that scenario, but he held me and waited for your command. That's very impressive."

Faith smiled at Turk. "He is a good dog."

The door opened again, and the three of them turned to see the uniform leading a protesting Gaucho down the path to the cruiser. Garvey and Michael approached them, holstering their weapons when they saw the situation under control.

When Garvey arrived, Eric said, "I'm sorry about your officer. I hope I didn't hurt him too badly."

His tone carried no hint of sarcasm, and Faith felt another pang at the knowledge that she would have to jail this man.

"He'll be fine," Garvey said with a wry smile. "He's not too happy with you right now. That's why I sent him down with Jimenez."

Eric lowered his head and nodded. "Yeah. I don't blame him." He lifted his head and looked at Michael. "Thank you," he said, "all of you. For stopping that dogfighting ring. I don't know if I would have been able to get to all of them. Definitely not before a lot more dogs were killed."

Faith didn't know what to say. Garvey seemed equally at a loss.

Fortunately, Turk and Michael had an idea. Michael met Eric's eyes and said, "It was my pleasure."

Turk walked to Eric and pressed against his leg, looking up at him with the sympathetic brown eyes that had won Faith's heart more than two years ago. Eric looked down at him and smiled. The pain behind that smile brought tears to Faith's eyes.

"What's his name?" Eric asked.

"Turk," Faith replied.

“Turk,” Eric repeated. “Good boy, Turk.”

***

Faith wasn't sure what to say. Normally, when she interviewed killers after apprehending them, she would ask them why they did what they did. This time, she knew exactly why Eric Ciccolo killed those men.

In the end, Eric spoke first. “I had a Shepherd too. She was a Husky mix, but only twelve percent. All she got from that side was the blue eyes and a love of snow.” He grinned. “I took her to Aspen once. The only time she ever disobeyed me was when I told her it was time to leave. She pretended not to hear me until I walked right up to her and gave her the parental, ‘I know you heard me’ look. God, she was a great dog. She wasn’t officially mine, of course. I just kept an eye on her when she or her handler was on vacation. That wasn’t really allowed, but they made an exception for me. I used to train a lot of dogs for PD. But you know that, I guess.”

Faith smiled sadly. “I’m sorry for your loss. I almost lost Turk too.”

Eric nodded sympathetically. "I'm glad you didn't. It's the worst thing in the world, short of losing a child. Maybe not everyone sees it that way, but I do." He shook his head. "I don't get it. I don't understand people who hurt dogs. Dogs are the most wonderful creatures on Earth. What possible entertainment do you get out of watching them die? I can understand that psychopaths exist, but the spectators?" he shook his head. "It's just obscene."

Faith couldn’t agree more. “Yes,” she said, “that’s the right word for it.”

“You know, I wasn’t going to do anything about it,” he said, “at first, anyway. I was just going to file the police report and leave it at that. Then I started doing some research. Did you know that over sixteen thousand dogs die each year in dog fights in the U.S. alone?”

Faith’s eyes widened. “No, I didn’t.”

"Yep," he said, "sixteen thousand every year. It's insane. All of those dogs killed just so people can see blood. Well, I couldn't stop all of them, but I could stop some of them. I thought that maybe if people were made aware of the issue ,it might inspire them to put an end to it. I think I was just being naïve, to be honest. People don't seem to care about anything that isn't directly affecting them."

“I’ve found that to be the case,” Faith replied. She thought of David, who insisted that West was no more of a threat to him than he was to anyone else and willfully ignored all of Faith’s protests to the contrary. She thought of Ellie, who similarly refused to leave, stubbornly holding on to the illusion of self-determination by defying a threat that she, of all people, should know was very real.

She thought of herself, who several times over the past two years had placed Turk, Michael, Gordon, the Boss and the Bureau in general at risk because of her impatience with the West case. People were born with blinders, she often thought. It was hard to remove those blinders, and when they did, it was just as hard to keep them off.

"So, do you know what happens next with me?" Eric asked.

“You’ll be charged with murder,” she said, “three counts felony murder and one count attempted murder. In addition, three counts trespassing, two breaking and entering, resisting arrest, assault on a peace officer, and because of the method of death, you’ll get enhancements on the murders.”

“Ouch,” he said, “so I’m in prison for life then.”

“Most likely,” Faith said. “You might get some consideration for the fact that your victims were violent criminals and for the fact that your dog was killed and that prompted you down this path, but more likely than not, you’ll end up in jail for the rest of your life. I’m sorry.”

“Don’t be,” he replied. “I knew this was coming. I knew it the moment I went after Harris. I made my peace with it.”

Faith once more didn’t know what to say. Her thoughts were at war with each other. The agent in her insisted that there was no excuse for what he had done. Murder was murder was killing someone illegally. It didn’t matter what the victims had done. There were laws and processes to follow, and when you didn’t follow them, bad things happened.

The human in her was very well acquainted with her own loose attitude concerning laws and processes in the past and understood precisely how someone could be willing to throw away everything for a chance at justice. *There but for the grace of God go I*, she thought.

“You’ll end up in medium security at first,” she said, “minimum after a few years of good behavior. You’ll get your own room and maybe even a tv if you make nice with the right CO’s. It might help to think of it as early retirement to an assisted living community.”

That sounded weak to her own ears, but Eric smiled and nodded. “Yeah, that’s how I’ll look at it. I think you might be a little optimistic about the timeline, though. I didn’t just shoot people. I shocked them to death with a collar. Unless every single one of the jurors is an avid dog lover and the judge owns a dog himself, I'll probably spend a while in max before I get an easier ride. But that's okay too. Even max has libraries. I've always been a reader. I can make it work."

For the third time in their conversation, Faith didn't know what to say. Eric looked at Turk, who sat next to Faith, sympathy in his brown eyes.

"You take care of your mommy, you hear?" he said. "She loves you very much."

A lump formed in Faith's throat. She stood and broke about a half dozen protocols when she shook Eric's hand—as much as the shackles around his wrists would allow—and said, "Good luck, Eric. I hope you find the peace you're looking for."

"I've already found it," he replied.

CHAPTER TWENTY FOUR

"How's Gaucho doing?" Michael asked when Garvey returned to the agents with a pitcher of beer.

Garvey had offered to treat them to drinks before they returned to Philadelphia. The earlier tension between them was forgotten now that the case was solved and Garvey didn't risk losing her traction against the Georgia Syndicate.

"Gaucho is doing beautifully," Garvey replied. "Roman and the others might have what they think of as honor among thieves, but Gaucho here has the decency to admit that it's all about him. He's been singing like Pavarotti. I can't say his voice is as pretty, but he's telling me everything I need to hear, so I'll buy the record when it comes out."

"He's really throwing everyone under the bus, huh?" Michael asked, a touch of contempt in his voice.

Faith lifted an eyebrow. "And that upsets you?"

"Oh, not at all," Michael said, "Put me on the waiting list for that album too. I just enjoy thinking about what a little coward he turned out to be. It makes it easier for me to get over what I saw in that warehouse. Speaking of which, what happened to the dogs?"

Garvey looked at Faith. Michael's smile faded. "Gone, huh?"

"Not all of them," Garvey said. "It looks like about half of them survived the firefight. Gaucho was responsible for killing them, but he ended up fleeing before the job was done. The ones that survived, though… well, they're not going back home."

Faith and Michael nodded soberly. What those dogs had been put through had warped and hurt them to the point where they could no longer be safely returned to their owners. "What's going to happen to them?" Faith asked.

"Ciccolo recommended a trainer he knows," Garvey replied. "There's a guy on the West Coast who takes in dogs that have been psychologically damaged and gives them a place to live out their days that's safe for them and safe for people. They'll be shipped there. I looked at some pictures. It's pretty nice. He's got sixty acres in the Los Angeles Mountains. They'll get to run around and play and forget all about the assholes who wanted them to fight and kill each other."

“That’s good,” Faith said, “that’s a lot better than it could have been.”

“Yeah,” Garvey agreed. “If we hadn’t found a place for them, they would have all been euthanized. Makes me wonder if we’re really that much better than the Syndicate is.”

“We are,” Michael said firmly. “It’s not even close.”

Faith had a feeling that Garvey wasn’t being serious about the comparison, but Garvey didn’t challenge Michael. Faith looked at her partner and saw a very familiar anger in his face. She couldn’t imagine his experience would affect him as long as her suffering at Trammell’s and West’s hands would affect her, but she had a pretty good idea what he was feeling right now.

“So what’s next for you?” Michael asked Garvey after a moment of silence. “The city going to give you a medal for taking out the Syndicate?”

Garvey chuckled. “I wish. Not the medal part. They actually might give me a medal, the knuckleheads. They’ll almost certainly promote me to Detective Sergeant. Hell, they might even leapfrog me to lieutenant. But no, the Syndicate isn’t dead. This hurt them, but not badly enough to stop them. They’ll be back, and things will be worse when they return.”

“It can’t be that bad,” Faith said. “You’ve shown that the police department here won’t take their actions lightly. You’ll be able to argue for more of a budget so you can step up patrols in the worst neighborhoods. You can even make some traction on social programs that will help people in lower income situations find alternative ways to support themselves. You’ll make a difference.”

"Everything you've said is true," Garvey agreed, "but there will always be people who have less, and those people will always envy those who have more. There will always be those among the ones who have more who exploit those people to gain even more than they have, and there will be people all across the social strata who will be willing to do whatever it takes to get it. That's the human condition right there, and until and unless we evolve into something different, we'll always have groups like the Syndicate to fight.

“But there will always be people to fight them,” she added, “and as long as that’s the case, I’ll keep smiling.” She lifted her glass and said, “To our victory.”

“To victory,” Michael agreed.

“To victory,” Faith said softly.

***

Hello, you have reached—"Dr. David Friedman"*—We're sorry, but—*"Dr. David Friedman"*—is not available. At the tone, please record your message. When you have finished, press pound.*

The tone beeped and Faith said, "Hey, David, it's me. I just wanted to let you know that we're on our way home. We should be there tonight. We're landing at—" she checked her itinerary "—nine-thirty. You don't have to meet me at the airport or anything. I'll be too tired to do anything anyway. Not that I'm asking you to do anything." She reddened slightly and said, "Anyway, I'm just calling to let you know. If you're available tomorrow night, though, I'd love to grab dinner. I… um… I have a thought on the… situation."

She reddened even further and wondered how she was going to broach the subject with David. She had given up on David leaving the state until things were settled with West. Considering how easily West managed to move around the country and track even Faith's most obscure acquaintances, she thought David might be right after all, even if indirectly. It probably didn't matter where he went. West could find him if he wanted to.

But she could still make things safer for him if she were with him as much as possible. She wasn't planning to move in with him permanently. Not yet, anyway. Just until West was caught. True, she hadn't really had the best showings against West in their fights, and neither had Turk, but David stood a much better chance with her and Turk there than not.

But it would probably come across as paranoia or clinginess when she brought the idea up to David. She wasn't sure which was worse.

"Anyway," she finished, "you're probably busy at work, so I'll let you go. I'll see you soon." She hesitated briefly, then said, "I love you."

"I love you too," Michael said.

Faith turned around in surprise, then saw that Michael was also on the phone. "I'll see you soon, beautiful," he said. He paused, then blushed a little and said, "Well, that sounds just fantastic. I can't wait to see you in it."

Faith turned around so Michael wouldn't see her smile. Unless Michael's tastes had changed greatly over the past few years, she had a decent idea what Ellie was planning to wear for him.

She reddened and pushed that thought from her mind. She had no business going there and no real desire to go there anyway. They were partners and friends, and she was having enough trouble maintaining that relationship without allowing their past dalliance to complicate things.

Besides, she had another man to wear lingerie for. It occurred to her that she hadn't done that for David yet. Maybe she would buy something lacy and red for him and ask him about staying together once he'd had a chance to enjoy that outfit.

Michael hung up and sat next to her with a groan. "I'm getting too old for this shit," he said seriously. "I don't know how many more of these I have left in me."

"You're thinking about moving up?" Faith asked.

He hesitated a split second before saying, "Yeah, maybe."

Faith's eyes widened. "You're thinking about moving out?"

He shrugged. "Not soon. I don't even get my pension for another five years. But… well, I can't do this forever. It's starting to get to me, and not just physically. That dog fighting ring… I don't know, Faith. I've never felt so… helpless before. And what Garvey said about their always being people like the Syndicate… it makes me wonder if I'm just playing a fool's game thinking I can make an actual difference in the world."

"Everyone has to play this game, Michael," Faith said. "The only thing you get to choose is what side you're on."

"See, that's where you're wrong," Michael said gently. "You can decide to be an NPC."

"An NP-what?"

"NPC," he repeated. "It's a video game term. It means Non-Playable Character. You know in role-playing games how you have characters you interact with like teammates or shop owners or guides?"

Faith hadn't played video games since Super Nintendo was the state of the art. "Not really," she said, "but I think I get what you're saying."

"Yeah, well, sometimes I think it wouldn't be a bad idea to toss my gloves in the ring."

"You're using a lot of metaphors," Faith said.

He chuckled. "Bottom line is I'm going to be forty soon, and I'm starting to feel my age. Not just physically, but mentally and emotionally. I don't think I can be in this line of work as long as the Boss has. Don't tell him I said this, but there are days when I think *he* shouldn't have been here as long as he has."

"I don't know if it matters how long someone *should* be in our line of work. The work has to be done, and people have to do it. That's just the way it is."

"True," he said, "but maybe it's time for me to let someone else do it."

They fell silent a moment. Faith knew that Michael's potential retirement wouldn't come for a long time. He would stay long enough to get his pension for sure.

But he might not stay in the field.

She risked asking that question. "Are you going to leave the field?"

He didn't answer right away, which was as much answer as Faith needed. When he did answer, his voice sounded every bit as tired as he claimed to be. "Probably," he said, "not soon, but not forever from now, either. I don't know, man, I look at the Boss and I wonder when the last time he smiled—really smiled—was. Unless his personality is truly just an act that he's maintained religiously for the past thirty or so years, I don't think I've ever seen him happy. Desrouleaux's starting to get there too. I know the West case is helping that process along, but he's getting noticeably crabbier and slower and more tired. Chavez used to be able to cheer him up, but they're looking more and more like a cranky old man and his bubbly daughter." He chuckled. "I should tell him that. He'd get a kick out of that."

His smile faded again. "Garvey too. She's well on her way to being too cynical to see the positive in anything. And Jones from Idaho, the sheriff from Morgan County—I forget his name—they're all just bitter and cynical. I don't want to end up like them," he said. "Especially the Boss. I don't know what keeps him going. I sometimes think he just keeps going to give himself something to do besides drink."

"Does he drink?" Faith asked.

"Probably," Michael replied. "I don't know for sure, but I don't know how he'd make it through the nights without something to take the edge off. You know, you and I stress out about our cases, a few dead bodies here and there. I'm not belittling that at all, but have you ever thought about what it's like to be a SAC? They have to think about everything. Not just the murders even. Did you know that the Philadelphia Field Office has busted eight human trafficking rings and six counterfeit rings since the Boss took over?"

Faith's eyes widened. "No, I didn't."

"Yeah. I was looking through some of the old records one day out of curiosity. We never think about what the other divisions do, but there's some dark stuff going on in the world, and we only see a tiny corner of it. I don't know if I can handle seeing any more of it. And when I think of all the field offices in the country, all dealing more or less with the same stuff we're dealing with… well, I can see why some people end up succumbing to depression."

Faith didn't like where this conversation was going. "Michael, you can't tell me you think it's all for nothing."

"It's not," he said, "and I'm not saying it is. You know about the starfish analogy, right?"

"I don't think so," she said.

"I'll give you the abridged version. A guy finds a bunch of starfish washed up on a beach. The starfish are alive, but they have no chance of making it back to the water before they suffocate. So the guy walks along, and he comes to a little kid who's picking up the starfish one by one and tossing them back into the sea. The guy says, 'Kid, you're wasting your time. You'll never save all of them.' The kid picks up a starfish, throws it into the water, looks at the guy and says, 'I saved that one.' So I know it's not for nothing. There are little girls whose dogs won't be stolen and murdered in a ring now. There are people who will live because the killers we've captured won't be there to murder them anymore. That's a good thing. I just don't know if it's enough for me anymore."

"Exactly," Faith agreed with a smile. "That's why I keep going. I'm not stupid enough to think that stopping West is going to end all murder, but it will end some of them. Some people will get to live. That's what I mean by choosing what side you're on. I'd rather fight for the light than fight for the darkness, if you'll permit me to be cheesy."

She expected Michael to make some crack about her being cheesy, but he didn't. Instead, he said, "That's one thing I've come to admire about you, Faith. Even at your worst, you always have hope. I don't know if I do anymore."

The gate agent announced their boarding group before Faith could reply. Michael stood and smiled down at her. "You ready, kid?" he said.

"After you, old man," she replied, managing a smile despite the turmoil in her heart.

They boarded the plane, and Michael quickly closed his eyes and fell asleep. Or at least pretended to be asleep. He might not be in the mood for another Faith Bold pep talk, and for once, Faith didn't blame him.

She had planned to talk to him about helping her find West, but it clearly wasn't the right time to bring up the conversation. She would wait until tomorrow, until after he'd had a chance to see Ellie. Then he might be more receptive.

Try as she might, though, she couldn't shake the feeling that each day she delayed hunting West increased the chances that she'd wake up the next day to find someone she loved dead.

CHAPTER TWENTY FIVE

At nine-twenty-two pm, a man who was identified as Landon Guthrie watched Faith Bold and Michael Prince disembark from the airplane six rows ahead of him. Their dog, a handsome German Shepherd who was just beginning to show signs of aging, turned and fixed him with a pleasant smile.

Guthrie found it fascinating that dogs could smile. It amazed him the power that humans held over the rest of the world, power they didn't even realize. There were killer whales that would flee humans on sight, even though they had never seen humans before. They fled because their parents taught them to flee, how, scientists were still unsure. Killer whales, by far the most powerful marine predator the world had ever seen, would flee on sight from weak, hairless terrestrial apes.

And they had good reason to. Those apes had learned thousands of years ago how to refine metal out of ore and how to forge that metal into large pointy sticks that could with one well-guided throw—or, a few thousand years later, be shot from another tool humans had forged—could overcome their eight thousand pounds of muscle and a bite force many times greater than any creature alive, even when there were dozens of such animals and only a few of the weak little apes.

And wolves, among the most successful of terrestrial predators, smaller than orcas but just as cunning, had been bred by those same medium-sized apes into fiercely loyal slaves that actually mimicked their masters.

Humans truly were evolution's greatest achievement. And they were still so stupid that it sickened him.

Faith had made eye contact with him twice, once when he sat across from her in the boarding area and once when he passed her to take his seat. Michael had even smiled and nodded at him. What on Earth did Ellie see in him?

Well, Ellie wasn't any smarter than they were. She had lived for twelve years with him and had never suspected what he was. Even when she left, she hadn't suspected.

He was more worried about the dog. Turk might be a fiercely loyal slave, but he retained a larger helping of his ancestors' cunning than most slaves. He had gone to great lengths to alter his appearance, scent and mannerisms, but the man once known as Franklin West wasn't sure if that would be enough. Turk was, in many ways, even more dangerous than his master.

But the dog had only smiled before allowing Faith to lead him from the plane, his happy little subservient tail wagging cheerfully as they descended the jetbridge.

He stood, taking care to move slowly as a man of his age would. One of the flight attendants smiled at him as she stood on her tiptoes and handed him his luggage. "There you go, sir," she said, "have a safe trip home."

He smiled at her. “Thank you, sweetheart,” he said.

She gave him the tolerant smile that young women give sweet old men who aren’t aware that their word choice is problematic and said, “Good night, Mr. Guthrie.”

“Good night, sweetheart,” West replied.

***

Two hours later, West parked kady-corner to a quaint little Georgian-style rowhouse owned by one Dr. David Friedman, DVM. He eased himself out of the front seat of his small crossover SUV and walked tiredly up the steps to his own rowhouse, a rental unit that Landon Guthrie had reserved for the week. He walked inside and just as slowly took a seat on the easy chair in the living room. The curtains blocked the view from outside, but the small camera placed on the sill had a clear view of David's house and fed the image to West's cell phone.

The light was on in David’s window. That was good. It meant he could stay where he was and receive the answer to his question without putting himself at risk.

As he waited, he wondered who would be watching David. He had seen the FBI van when he arrived. They had put only a token effort into camouflaging it, painting it a shade of white and tinting the windows far past the legally permitted twenty percent.

But who was inside it? That was the question. Not Faith, obviously, nor her partner. Probably not Chavez or Desrouleaux either. They would be floating and overseeing. Rosa? Probably. Not alone, though. A more experienced agent would be supervising.

West wished he had spent more time studying Faith's field office. He was familiar with the major players and he knew about Chavez and Rosa from Faith, but there was a crowd of agents with whom West was unfamiliar, mediocre agents who would never do anything of real consequence as investigators but who were perfectly well suited to the job of looking at something.

Well, it didn't matter. West wouldn't be coming in through any entrance that the FBI could see, and when he did enter, he would make sure to wait until the light was off in David's window.

The FBI's response was admirable but entirely predictable. They had done exactly as he intended. They had requested a list of every name Faith had mentioned to him during their sessions, and Faith had dutifully provided that list.

Then the FBI had followed procedure. It was a good procedure. They would offer surveillance to everyone on the list. If West showed his face anywhere near one of them, he would be immediately apprehended.

It was a good plan except for one fatal flaw. They expected him to show his face. It never occurred to them that he could make his way into someone's house without showing his face.

But first, he had to make sure that David was alone. It was Faith's first night back from a case, and there was a greater than even chance that she would spend the night here. If so, he would simply wait until a night when he was alone.

He waited, and after twenty minutes, got his answer. A shadow—a male shadow—passed in front of the window and sat in front of the tv. Twenty more minutes passed, and the man didn't move, and West was now sure that David was alone in the house.

West placed his cell phone on the table and headed to the kitchen to make dinner. Tonight was the night, then.

Two hours later, David shut his tv off and got up. He walked out of view of the window and switched the light off. West waited one hour more, then removed his prosthetics and dressed in a black shirt and dark jeans. He pulled a black beanie over his head and left through the back door.

It took him fifteen minutes to make the journey around the neighborhood to end up behind David's house. He saw no sign of additional surveillance, which made sense. The FBI was always busy, and a lot of resources were being devoted to finding him. They didn't have enough manpower to station eyes at every corner.

But why would they? Even if West went in through the back door, he would have to walk down the street to get to David's house.

Except he didn't. He scanned the neighborhood as he walked and saw dark, shuttered windows. No one was on the street, and the dogs—if there were any—were sleeping.

He stopped in front of the small gap between buildings and shimmied into it. This would be the most difficult part.

He stopped behind the fence that walled off David's modest backyard from the equally modest backyard of the rowhouse directly behind it. West glanced toward David's street to make sure the FBI van was out of view, then starfished his way up the fence, pressing his back against the fence behind him and working his way up the fence in front of him. When he reached the top, he dropped quietly to the turf beneath.

He didn't bother being careful anymore, other than to quietly force the lock on David's back door. The FBI couldn't see him, and David would be dead before they could hear him.

He made his way up the stairs to David's bedroom. He smiled at the man's sleeping form and imagined how Faith would feel when she realized that she would never again feel that form next to her own.

He switched on the light.

David frowned, then stirred. He opened his eyes, blinking in confusion at the lighted room. His eyes drifted toward West. They hung on him for a moment, then suddenly focused.

David sat bolt upright and opened his mouth to cry out, but West reached him first.

EPILOGUE

The next morning, Faith decided she didn't want to wait to see David. He hadn't answered his phone the night before. That didn't necessarily mean anything. Even when they were in their first honeymoon phase, before everything got complicated, David hadn't been the best at answering his phone, but with everything going on and West active again, she didn't want to take any chances.

She called him as she dressed, and when he didn't answer again, she started to think the silence might mean something after all.

Relax, she told herself. *It's already nine. He's probably at work.*

Faith had slept in, exhausted from the case the night before. She expected to wake up to a good morning text from David, and when she didn't receive one, a seed of doubt began to sprout in her mind.

That seed was now a decent-sized sapling and growing fast. Faith rushed to get Turk ready and left.

She headed for David's work first. For a long time after today, this fact would haunt her, even though it wouldn't have changed anything had she gone to his house first.

And why shouldn't she go to his work? It was business hours, and David had made it clear how dedicated he was to his job. Of course, he would be at the office.

She stopped for coffee on the way. The line at Morning Glory was long, and Faith told herself that the relief she felt at that was just so she could spend more time thinking of something special she could order him. She even managed to convince herself that the decision to buy him a Mocha Latte with an extra shot of espresso was worthy of the careful deliberation she gave it.

This is stupid. He's at work. He has to be.

Faith had heard the grieving families of many victims say aloud the words that she now thought.

But she wasn't a grieving victim! David was alive! He was at work!

In the seat next to her, Turk—sensing Faith's anxiety—whined softly. She smiled at him and ruffled his fur. "It's all right, boy. We're just bringing David some coffee and saying hi."

And that was all. She would give him some coffee, talk with him a little bit, and flirt with him a little bit. She would tease him about the lingerie she was going to wear for him tonight, then she would go and buy the lingerie and some wine and chocolates and other finger foods that went well with romance. She would think of two movies for them to watch—a war movie for herself and a comedy for David—and she would shower and shave and put on her lingerie and put on her makeup and do her hair, and they would spend a night just enjoying each other.

Everything was going to be okay.

"Miss Bold?"

Faith blinked and smiled at the receptionist, a twenty-something named Denise with a perky smile and perkier hair. "I'm sorry, yes. Is David here?"

Denise shook her head and said with all the tact of someone whose biggest concern in life was what shoes she would wear to the club tonight, "No, I just told you. David hasn't been in today."

An alarm bell went off in Faith's mind. "Oh. Did he say why?"

"No. No one's been able to get a hold of him. We thought he was with you, honestly."

The floor dropped from under Faith. She gripped the edge of the counter to keep herself upright. "Oh," she said tonelessly. "All right."

Denise smiled uncertainly at Faith and looked incredibly relieved when Faith turned to leave. Turk whined and looked back at David's office door, then back at Faith.

"Come on, boy," she said in that same toneless voice. "David's home."

She didn't speed on the way to David's house. She didn't break the limit once. That was another fact that would haunt her, even though she knew as she drove that she was too late. What was done was done.

But nothing was done. Of course, nothing was done. They had just gotten back together. There was no way he was d—wasn't home.

She parked in front of his rowhouse and got out of her car, heading up the steps in a half-run. She heard scratching behind her and turned to see she had left Turk in the car.

She laughed, a brittle, metallic sound like the shattering of a crystal glass and trotted back to her car. She would have to buy a car with automatic unlock so she could just let him out with a click of the button next time.

As she opened the door, she caught sight of herself in the mirror. Her eyes were opened wide, her lips pressed together, her face pale.

She saw the fear in her eyes, but worse than the fear was the knowledge.

She opened the door. Turk bolted toward David's house, but Faith called for him to stop and come to her. He looked at her, saw the knowledge in her eyes and revealed the knowledge in his.

She ascended the steps unhurriedly. There was no point in hurrying. She pressed the doorbell more out of rote reflex than out of intentional delay.

There was no answer. She didn't bother pressing it again. She knelt down and began picking the lock. It clicked open just as a voice behind her said, "Hey! Excuse me!"

"It's me, Special Agent Tiller," Faith said.

"Bold?" Tiller said, furrowing his brow. "Why are you picking the lock? I thought you had a key."

"I was going to ask him for one today," she said numbly.

Tiller closed the distance and saw her expression. "Is everything all right?" he asked.

In answer, Faith simply opened the door.

NOW AVAILABLE!

SO SIMPLE
(A Faith Bold Mystery—Book 11)

Victims of a new killer are found dead, the only thing linking them that they are dog owners. As FBI Special Agent Faith Bold navigates the world of dog shelters, her K9 German Shepherd, Turk, at her side, she realizes something is awry—and that, as she heads into a trap, she just may need Turk to catch the killer—and to save her life….

"A masterpiece of thriller and mystery."
—Books and Movie Reviews, Roberto Mattos (re Once Gone)

SO SIMPLE is Book #11 in a long-anticipated new series by #1 bestseller and USA Today bestselling author Blake Pierce, whose bestseller Once Gone (a free download) has received over 7,000 five star ratings and reviews.

FBI Special Agent Faith Bold doesn't believe she can ever return to the force after the trauma she's been through. Suffering from past demons, she feels unfit for duty and content to retire—until Turk walks into her life.

Turk, a former Marine Corps dog, wounded in battle, suffers from his own demons. But he never lets it show as he gives everything to Faith to get her back on her feet.

Each are slow to warm up to each other, but when they do, they are inseparable. Each is equally determined to hunt down the demons chasing them, whatever the cost, and to watch each other's backs—even at the risk of their own life.

A page-turning and harrowing crime thriller featuring a brilliant and tortured FBI agent, the Faith Bold series is a riveting mystery, packed with non-stop action, suspense, twists and turns, revelations, and driven by a breakneck pace that will keep you flipping pages late into the night. Fans of Rachel Caine, Teresa Driscoll and Robert Dugoni are sure to fall in love.

Future books in the series are now also available.

“An edge of your seat thriller in a new series that keeps you turning pages! ...So many twists, turns and red herrings… I can't wait to see what happens next.”
—Reader review (Her Last Wish)

“A strong, complex story about two FBI agents trying to stop a serial killer. If you want an author to capture your attention and have you guessing, yet trying to put the pieces together, Pierce is your author!”
—Reader review (Her Last Wish)

“A typical Blake Pierce twisting, turning, roller coaster ride suspense thriller. Will have you turning the pages to the last sentence of the last chapter!!!”
—Reader review (City of Prey)

“Right from the start we have an unusual protagonist that I haven't seen done in this genre before. The action is nonstop… A very atmospheric novel that will keep you turning pages well into the wee hours.”
—Reader review (City of Prey)

“Everything that I look for in a book… a great plot, interesting characters, and grabs your interest right away. The book moves along at a breakneck pace and stays that way until the end. Now on go I to book two!”
—Reader review (Girl, Alone)

“Exciting, heart pounding, edge of your seat book… a must read for mystery and suspense readers!”
—Reader review (Girl, Alone)

Blake Pierce

Blake Pierce is the USA Today bestselling author of the RILEY PAGE mystery series, which includes seventeen books. Blake Pierce is also the author of the MACKENZIE WHITE mystery series, comprising fourteen books; of the AVERY BLACK mystery series, comprising six books; of the KERI LOCKE mystery series, comprising five books; of the MAKING OF RILEY PAIGE mystery series, comprising six books; of the KATE WISE mystery series, comprising seven books; of the CHLOE FINE psychological suspense mystery, comprising six books; of the JESSIE HUNT psychological suspense thriller series, comprising thirty-five books (and counting); of the AU PAIR psychological suspense thriller series, comprising three books; of the ZOE PRIME mystery series, comprising six books; of the ADELE SHARP mystery series, comprising sixteen books, of the EUROPEAN VOYAGE cozy mystery series, comprising six books; of the LAURA FROST FBI suspense thriller, comprising eleven books; of the ELLA DARK FBI suspense thriller, comprising twenty-one books (and counting); of the A YEAR IN EUROPE cozy mystery series, comprising nine books, of the AVA GOLD mystery series, comprising six books; of the RACHEL GIFT mystery series, comprising thirteen books (and counting); of the VALERIE LAW mystery series, comprising nine books; of the PAIGE KING mystery series, comprising eight books; of the MAY MOORE mystery series, comprising eleven books; of the CORA SHIELDS mystery series, comprising eight books; of the NICKY LYONS mystery series, comprising eight books, of the CAMI LARK mystery series, comprising ten books; of the AMBER YOUNG mystery series, comprising seven books (and counting); of the DAISY FORTUNE mystery series, comprising five books; of the FIONA RED mystery series, comprising eleven books (and counting); of the FAITH BOLD mystery series, comprising eleven books (and counting); of the JULIETTE HART mystery series, comprising five books (and counting); of the MORGAN CROSS mystery series, comprising nine books (and counting); of the FINN WRIGHT mystery series, comprising five books (and counting); of the new SHEILA STONE suspense thriller series, comprising five books (and counting); and of the new RACHEL BLACKWOOD suspense thriller series, comprising five books (and counting).

An avid reader and lifelong fan of the mystery and thriller genres, Blake loves to hear from you, so please feel free to visit www.blakepierceauthor.com to learn more and stay in touch.

BOOKS BY BLAKE PIERCE

RACHEL BLACKWOOD SUSPENSE THRILLER

NOT THIS WAY (Book #1)
NOT THIS TIME (Book #2)
NOT THIS CLOSE (Book #3)
NOT THIS ROAD (Book #4)
NOT THIS LATE (Book #5)

SHEILA STONE SUSPENSE THRILLER

SILENT GIRL (Book #1)
SILENT TRAIL (Book #2)
SILENT NIGHT (Book #3)
SILENT HOUSE (Book #4)
SILENT SCREAM (Book #5)

FINN WRIGHT MYSTERY SERIES

WHEN YOU'RE MINE (Book #1)
WHEN YOU'RE SAFE (Book #2)
WHEN YOU'RE CLOSE (Book #3)
WHEN YOU'RE SLEEPING (Book #4)
WHEN YOU'RE SANE (Book #5)

MORGAN CROSS MYSTERY SERIES

FOR YOU (Book #1)
FOR RAGE (Book #2)
FOR LUST (Book #3)
FOR WRATH (Book #4)
FOREVER (Book #5)
FOR US (Book #6)
FOR NOW (Book #7)
FOR ONCE (Book #8)
FOR ETERNITY (Book #9)

JULIETTE HART MYSTERY SERIES

NOTHING TO FEAR (Book #1)
NOTHING THERE (Book #2)

NOTHING WATCHING (Book #3)
NOTHING HIDING (Book #4)
NOTHING LEFT (Book #5)

FAITH BOLD MYSTERY SERIES
SO LONG (Book #1)
SO COLD (Book #2)
SO SCARED (Book #3)
SO NORMAL (Book #4)
SO FAR GONE (Book #5)
SO LOST (Book #6)
SO ALONE (Book #7)
SO FORGOTTEN (Book #8)
SO INSANE (Book #9)
SO SMITTEN (Book #10)
SO SIMPLE (Book #11)

FIONA RED MYSTERY SERIES
LET HER GO (Book #1)
LET HER BE (Book #2)
LET HER HOPE (Book #3)
LET HER WISH (Book #4)
LET HER LIVE (Book #5)
LET HER RUN (Book #6)
LET HER HIDE (Book #7)
LET HER BELIEVE (Book #8)
LET HER FORGET (Book #9)
LET HER TRY (Book #10)
LET HER PLAY (Book #11)

DAISY FORTUNE MYSTERY SERIES
NEED YOU (Book #1)
CLAIM YOU (Book #2)
CRAVE YOU (Book #3)
CHOOSE YOU (Book #4)
CHASE YOU (Book #5)

AMBER YOUNG MYSTERY SERIES
ABSENT PITY (Book #1)
ABSENT REMORSE (Book #2)

ABSENT FEELING (Book #3)
ABSENT MERCY (Book #4)
ABSENT REASON (Book #5)
ABSENT SANITY (Book #6)
ABSENT LIFE (Book #7)

CAMI LARK MYSTERY SERIES
JUST ME (Book #1)
JUST OUTSIDE (Book #2)
JUST RIGHT (Book #3)
JUST FORGET (Book #4)
JUST ONCE (Book #5)
JUST HIDE (Book #6)
JUST NOW (Book #7)
JUST HOPE (Book #8)
JUST LEAVE (Book #9)
JUST TONIGHT (Book #10)

NICKY LYONS MYSTERY SERIES
ALL MINE (Book #1)
ALL HIS (Book #2)
ALL HE SEES (Book #3)
ALL ALONE (Book #4)
ALL FOR ONE (Book #5)
ALL HE TAKES (Book #6)
ALL FOR ME (Book #7)
ALL IN (Book #8)

CORA SHIELDS MYSTERY SERIES
UNDONE (Book #1)
UNWANTED (Book #2)
UNHINGED (Book #3)
UNSAID (Book #4)
UNGLUED (Book #5)
UNSTABLE (Book #6)
UNKNOWN (Book #7)
UNAWARE (Book #8)

MAY MOORE SUSPENSE THRILLER
NEVER RUN (Book #1)

NEVER TELL (Book #2)
NEVER LIVE (Book #3)
NEVER HIDE (Book #4)
NEVER FORGIVE (Book #5)
NEVER AGAIN (Book #6)
NEVER LOOK BACK (Book #7)
NEVER FORGET (Book #8)
NEVER LET GO (Book #9)
NEVER PRETEND (Book #10)
NEVER HESITATE (Book #11)

PAIGE KING MYSTERY SERIES
THE GIRL HE PINED (Book #1)
THE GIRL HE CHOSE (Book #2)
THE GIRL HE TOOK (Book #3)
THE GIRL HE WISHED (Book #4)
THE GIRL HE CROWNED (Book #5)
THE GIRL HE WATCHED (Book #6)
THE GIRL HE WANTED (Book #7)
THE GIRL HE CLAIMED (Book #8)

VALERIE LAW MYSTERY SERIES
NO MERCY (Book #1)
NO PITY (Book #2)
NO FEAR (Book #3)
NO SLEEP (Book #4)
NO QUARTER (Book #5)
NO CHANCE (Book #6)
NO REFUGE (Book #7)
NO GRACE (Book #8)
NO ESCAPE (Book #9)

RACHEL GIFT MYSTERY SERIES
HER LAST WISH (Book #1)
HER LAST CHANCE (Book #2)
HER LAST HOPE (Book #3)
HER LAST FEAR (Book #4)
HER LAST CHOICE (Book #5)
HER LAST BREATH (Book #6)
HER LAST MISTAKE (Book #7)

HER LAST DESIRE (Book #8)
HER LAST REGRET (Book #9)
HER LAST HOUR (Book #10)
HER LAST SHOT (Book #11)
HER LAST PRAYER (Book #12)
HER LAST LIE (Book #13)

AVA GOLD MYSTERY SERIES
CITY OF PREY (Book #1)
CITY OF FEAR (Book #2)
CITY OF BONES (Book #3)
CITY OF GHOSTS (Book #4)
CITY OF DEATH (Book #5)
CITY OF VICE (Book #6)

A YEAR IN EUROPE
A MURDER IN PARIS (Book #1)
DEATH IN FLORENCE (Book #2)
VENGEANCE IN VIENNA (Book #3)
A FATALITY IN SPAIN (Book #4)

ELLA DARK FBI SUSPENSE THRILLER
GIRL, ALONE (Book #1)
GIRL, TAKEN (Book #2)
GIRL, HUNTED (Book #3)
GIRL, SILENCED (Book #4)
GIRL, VANISHED (Book 5)
GIRL ERASED (Book #6)
GIRL, FORSAKEN (Book #7)
GIRL, TRAPPED (Book #8)
GIRL, EXPENDABLE (Book #9)
GIRL, ESCAPED (Book #10)
GIRL, HIS (Book #11)
GIRL, LURED (Book #12)
GIRL, MISSING (Book #13)
GIRL, UNKNOWN (Book #14)
GIRL, DECEIVED (Book #15)
GIRL, FORLORN (Book #16)
GIRL, REMADE (Book #17)
GIRL, BETRAYED (Book #18)

GIRL, BOUND (Book #19)
GIRL, REFORMED (Book #20)
GIRL, REBORN (Book #21)

LAURA FROST FBI SUSPENSE THRILLER
ALREADY GONE (Book #1)
ALREADY SEEN (Book #2)
ALREADY TRAPPED (Book #3)
ALREADY MISSING (Book #4)
ALREADY DEAD (Book #5)
ALREADY TAKEN (Book #6)
ALREADY CHOSEN (Book #7)
ALREADY LOST (Book #8)
ALREADY HIS (Book #9)
ALREADY LURED (Book #10)
ALREADY COLD (Book #11)

EUROPEAN VOYAGE COZY MYSTERY SERIES
MURDER (AND BAKLAVA) (Book #1)
DEATH (AND APPLE STRUDEL) (Book #2)
CRIME (AND LAGER) (Book #3)
MISFORTUNE (AND GOUDA) (Book #4)
CALAMITY (AND A DANISH) (Book #5)
MAYHEM (AND HERRING) (Book #6)

ADELE SHARP MYSTERY SERIES
LEFT TO DIE (Book #1)
LEFT TO RUN (Book #2)
LEFT TO HIDE (Book #3)
LEFT TO KILL (Book #4)
LEFT TO MURDER (Book #5)
LEFT TO ENVY (Book #6)
LEFT TO LAPSE (Book #7)
LEFT TO VANISH (Book #8)
LEFT TO HUNT (Book #9)
LEFT TO FEAR (Book #10)
LEFT TO PREY (Book #11)
LEFT TO LURE (Book #12)
LEFT TO CRAVE (Book #13)
LEFT TO LOATHE (Book #14)

LEFT TO HARM (Book #15)
LEFT TO RUIN (Book #16)

THE AU PAIR SERIES
ALMOST GONE (Book#1)
ALMOST LOST (Book #2)
ALMOST DEAD (Book #3)

ZOE PRIME MYSTERY SERIES
FACE OF DEATH (Book#1)
FACE OF MURDER (Book #2)
FACE OF FEAR (Book #3)
FACE OF MADNESS (Book #4)
FACE OF FURY (Book #5)
FACE OF DARKNESS (Book #6)

A JESSIE HUNT PSYCHOLOGICAL SUSPENSE SERIES
THE PERFECT WIFE (Book #1)
THE PERFECT BLOCK (Book #2)
THE PERFECT HOUSE (Book #3)
THE PERFECT SMILE (Book #4)
THE PERFECT LIE (Book #5)
THE PERFECT LOOK (Book #6)
THE PERFECT AFFAIR (Book #7)
THE PERFECT ALIBI (Book #8)
THE PERFECT NEIGHBOR (Book #9)
THE PERFECT DISGUISE (Book #10)
THE PERFECT SECRET (Book #11)
THE PERFECT FAÇADE (Book #12)
THE PERFECT IMPRESSION (Book #13)
THE PERFECT DECEIT (Book #14)
THE PERFECT MISTRESS (Book #15)
THE PERFECT IMAGE (Book #16)
THE PERFECT VEIL (Book #17)
THE PERFECT INDISCRETION (Book #18)
THE PERFECT RUMOR (Book #19)
THE PERFECT COUPLE (Book #20)
THE PERFECT MURDER (Book #21)
THE PERFECT HUSBAND (Book #22)
THE PERFECT SCANDAL (Book #23)

THE PERFECT MASK (Book #24)
THE PERFECT RUSE (Book #25)
THE PERFECT VENEER (Book #26)
THE PERFECT PEOPLE (Book #27)
THE PERFECT WITNESS (Book #28)
THE PERFECT APPEARANCE (Book #29)
THE PERFECT TRAP (Book #30)
THE PERFECT EXPRESSION (Book #31)
THE PERFECT ACCOMPLICE (Book #32)
THE PERFECT SHOW (Book #33)
THE PERFECT POISE (Book #34)
THE PERFECT CROWD (Book #35)

CHLOE FINE PSYCHOLOGICAL SUSPENSE SERIES
NEXT DOOR (Book #1)
A NEIGHBOR'S LIE (Book #2)
CUL DE SAC (Book #3)
SILENT NEIGHBOR (Book #4)
HOMECOMING (Book #5)
TINTED WINDOWS (Book #6)

KATE WISE MYSTERY SERIES
IF SHE KNEW (Book #1)
IF SHE SAW (Book #2)
IF SHE RAN (Book #3)
IF SHE HID (Book #4)
IF SHE FLED (Book #5)
IF SHE FEARED (Book #6)
IF SHE HEARD (Book #7)

THE MAKING OF RILEY PAIGE SERIES
WATCHING (Book #1)
WAITING (Book #2)
LURING (Book #3)
TAKING (Book #4)
STALKING (Book #5)
KILLING (Book #6)

RILEY PAIGE MYSTERY SERIES
ONCE GONE (Book #1)

ONCE TAKEN (Book #2)
ONCE CRAVED (Book #3)
ONCE LURED (Book #4)
ONCE HUNTED (Book #5)
ONCE PINED (Book #6)
ONCE FORSAKEN (Book #7)
ONCE COLD (Book #8)
ONCE STALKED (Book #9)
ONCE LOST (Book #10)
ONCE BURIED (Book #11)
ONCE BOUND (Book #12)
ONCE TRAPPED (Book #13)
ONCE DORMANT (Book #14)
ONCE SHUNNED (Book #15)
ONCE MISSED (Book #16)
ONCE CHOSEN (Book #17)

MACKENZIE WHITE MYSTERY SERIES
BEFORE HE KILLS (Book #1)
BEFORE HE SEES (Book #2)
BEFORE HE COVETS (Book #3)
BEFORE HE TAKES (Book #4)
BEFORE HE NEEDS (Book #5)
BEFORE HE FEELS (Book #6)
BEFORE HE SINS (Book #7)
BEFORE HE HUNTS (Book #8)
BEFORE HE PREYS (Book #9)
BEFORE HE LONGS (Book #10)
BEFORE HE LAPSES (Book #11)
BEFORE HE ENVIES (Book #12)
BEFORE HE STALKS (Book #13)
BEFORE HE HARMS (Book #14)

AVERY BLACK MYSTERY SERIES
CAUSE TO KILL (Book #1)
CAUSE TO RUN (Book #2)
CAUSE TO HIDE (Book #3)
CAUSE TO FEAR (Book #4)
CAUSE TO SAVE (Book #5)
CAUSE TO DREAD (Book #6)

KERI LOCKE MYSTERY SERIES

A TRACE OF DEATH (Book #1)

A TRACE OF MURDER (Book #2)

A TRACE OF VICE (Book #3)

A TRACE OF CRIME (Book #4)

A TRACE OF HOPE (Book #5)

Manufactured by Amazon.ca
Acheson, AB

12990855R00099